The Terranian Enigma
By
Andrew Dunkley

<u>Main Characters</u>

<u>The Andromedans</u>

Admiral Karlou Vardourn – First Andromedan Fleet, Commander of ISS Titania

Bishon Grudek – Supreme Leader

Yeovale Darnuth – First Officer, ISS Titania

Maneva Gantu – Ship's Medical Officer

Narrom Gish – Chief of the Watch

Captain Cion Zanaeus – Commander of ISS Vittorius

Arda Guz - Pilot

Miran Gase- Cadet

<u>The Terranians</u>

Filo – Technician and Amateur Astronomer

Sanita – Filo's wife

Jako – Astronomer

Barkou – President of the Astronomical Society

Ludic – Professor of Linguistics

<u>Terranian League of Governors</u>

Garon of Estonita

Percius of Eropa

Callon of Afrikaan

Marron of Pancifica

Bayou of Artesia

Vanis of Carthidge

<u>The Borche</u>

Galek – Clan Lord-Sennas Sector, Commander of the Quaal

<u>Acknowledgements</u>

Thanks to my wife Judy for proofreading the manuscript and tolerating my long-winded explanations of the plot and testing the twists in the storyline.

To my brother Steve, you are a graphics legend, thanks for the amazing cover!

Thanks to Professor Fred Watson for opening my mind to the possibilities of taking truth and turning it into Science Fiction.

Thanks also to the many Space Nuts Podcast listeners who pitched concepts for the book's title when I was devoid of ideas.

Dedicated to my Grandchildren, always let your imaginations run riot.

Chapter 1 – Prelude

After thousands of years and trillions of deaths, the planet had finally reached a state of peace. The people had endured seven world wars and thousands of other smaller conflicts, the consequences of which were catastrophic and without any semblance of logic. Life was extinguished at the whim of tyrants. For a very long time it seemed that intelligent life would fade away having achieved nothing but its own demise.

The early wars were fought over continents, the main antagonists seeking new territories for themselves. Later the wars were fought over ideology or conflicting religious beliefs but then the war for resources erupted. With the planet facing the threat of a runaway greenhouse effect, scientists and the leaders of nations argued over the remedy. While many agreed that the industrialisation of the planet had injected too many gases into the atmosphere, others ignored the warnings and kept poisoning the world. Those that united against them were forced to take drastic action and the Fifth World War began.

This conflict lasted nearly one hundred years, no-one willing to relent and, ironically, it further poisoned the atmosphere when the losing superpower in its dying gasp unleashed hundreds of nuclear warheads in a bid to extinguish the foe. They failed, with most of their missiles destroyed before they could reach their targets, exploding in the stratosphere. With the planet counting its losses, peace came again and lasted a thousand years, but the price was high with many nations facing significant economic turmoil. They were forced to make impossible decisions. With famine and disease ravaging their populations they allowed their governments to fold and handover their lands to bigger nations.

This was known as the War of Economics and was fought in houses of Government and Corporate headquarters rather than on battlefields. It saw the rich and powerful nations of the World racing once again for territory. Their leaders knew that the only way to maintain superiority was to be the biggest and nations that had held their own for millennia were suddenly extinct. Their people were forced into servitude as soldiers or slaves, most given menial tasks and treated no better than farm animals. When that war finally ended there were no more nations, just four continental superpowers, Chinaya: Europa, Oceania and the Southern Territories. All were equally powerful and all hell bent on being in total control.

For another thousand odd years there was an uneasy peace with occasional skirmishes over border issues, mainly with people fleeing one power hoping for a better life with another. They were always wrong. No one power cared for any of the migrants and ultimately, they were no better off. The vast majority lived pitiful, soulless lives.

Then in the year 7881, war erupted again. Chinaya had been secretly developing new super weapons. They had been exploring space and harvested new and exotic minerals from asteroids creating weapons that had no equal. They soon swept the planet, vanquishing Europa then Oceania. They were stopped in the Southern Territories, not by soldiers but by the geography and environment. By now the air had become so poisonous, venturing outside was impossible without body suits and respirators. The Southern Territorians took to living underground while the Chinayans retreated. The planet laid waste for the next five thousand years and the wars of the past became distant memories.

Interestingly the two superpowers remained resolute. There was no new migration of people seeking better lives or opportunities, no breakaway groups or political actions on either side. Each settled into their chosen lifestyles, which were demonstrably different.

As the planet healed itself the people began again to venture out, inevitably the Chinayans and Southern Territorians crossed paths again.

Initially it seemed like peace was possible, but the ideological differences were soon clear. Chinaya had settled on brutality as its form of governance which was unwavering. They killed anyone who stepped outside the legal bounds. There were only two levels of existence, the Elitists and the Slaveists. While an Elitist could become a Slaveist by breaking the law the opposite was impossible. Life in Chinaya was prosperous for a minority of the people, the majority living in fear and deprivation.

The Territorians, however, had reached an epoch. They saw life as a cooperative venture and endeavoured to stamp out poverty and hatred. It took them hundreds of years of re-education but ultimately, they achieved what they called

"Equilibrium". No-one wanted for anything. All were treated with respect and equality. Life was good.

When word of the Territorian ways filtered into the minds of the Slaveist Chinayans the results were catastrophic. The people rebelled against the Elitists, but they had no hope. Those that were not killed retreated to the Southern Territories and were taken in as refugees. When the Chinayan governors realised what had happened they attacked the Southern Territories. For a thousand days and nights they bombarded the Territorians with their super weapons to wipe them out. They then sent in ground troops to mop up.

The Territorians were fully aware of the tactic and they were prepared. Chinaya made a full commitment to the attack. They sent every man, every ship, every aircraft expecting to overrun the Territorians and achieve a swift victory. What they did not know was that the Territorians had built superior defences and none of the 1000-day blitz had anything more than a superficial effect. When the Chinayans arrived, they faced a motivated and angry foe and the war devolved into a siege.

Fighting was relentless and bloody and lasted years. Tens of millions died on both sides but, in time the will of the Territorians prevailed. They pushed back the Chinayan forces. Many of them surrendered, their spirits crushed. To their surprise they were treated fairly, fed and clothed and allowed to live. The realisation that their internment was better than life at home saw them negotiate with the Territorians and ultimately, they fought side by side to free their families from tyranny. Word of this saw more Chinayan troops defect. Eventually the Chinayan governors had barely a skeleton force to defend their soil. They fought to the death. The Seventh and final World War was over.

Over the next few thousand years the planet repaired itself yet again. The people became like-minded, lived for the planet rather than themselves. Things that were seen as unnecessary were discontinued, interplanetary exploration, deep ocean exploration and armaments. Things like astronomy became hobbies while science was primarily focused only on the betterment of life and longevity. There were exceptions, such as mining for metals to enhance technology but the pristine environment was always revived. All decisions were aimed at achieving global balance. No-one wanted for anything; there was no unemployment except for those who were frail or incapable of working. They were cared for. One language, one currency and one economy was developed. There were no nations, no religion and no one person was in power; a League of Governors, a democracy that followed a strict constitution that had been forged out of all that had gone wrong for so many years past. While there was still petty crime, minor disagreements and a need for a police force; armies, air forces and navies were disbanded, weapons of mass destruction themselves destroyed. The global effect of this peace was indescribable and the people rejoiced.

For another thousand years the people revelled in a life that none could have imagined. The planet's air cleared, scientists overcame all forms of disease so that being healthy and being long lived were just normal states. Yes, some people died accidentally or through misadventure, but overall life expectancy became much more significant, like no time in history. The people of what we now called Terrania lived in harmony. There was rarely, if ever a murder to speak of and prisons became unnecessary while hospitals were typically only used in times of emergency or accident. Schools became the major institutions that endured and education was free for everyone.

Over time everyone became used to this cooperative life of plenty and complacency spread silently through the generations. The only thing they didn't count on was another intervention, not of their making but from Space.

It was the 4th day of the second solar quarter in the year 13948...when they came.

Chapter 2 – The Discovery

Filo called to his wife, "I'm just going to the roof. It's a perfect night to observe!"

"Very good," replied Sanita, "Take your time, all is well with the children."

Filo was very excited; he'd never seen the sky so luminous. With the days of pollution and foul air long gone, the skies of Terrania were spectacularly clear and he wanted so much to make some kind of significant discovery and write a paper about it; perhaps winning a prize from the Amateur Astronomical Society for seeing something extraordinary and documenting it for the first time. Filo was a dreamer.

During the day he worked in the city as a computer technician, maintaining the city's vast quantum grid. It was mindless work a lot of the time as most of the technology was self-monitoring and self-repairing. He only needed to step in when something unforeseen occurred which was basically never. Terrania was a green power planet, only using renewables. Nuclear and coal power had been jettisoned long ago and, despite the time it took, the alternative energy program was now efficient and abundant. Filo's solace was astronomy and he was on the roof every other night watching the heavens when the weather permitted and tonight was indeed excellent, clear skies and moonless.

With the city's power grid turned down to the red scale to help people sleep, there was little in the way of light pollution to interfere with his view. Besides, the small quantum computer in the telescope was more than capable of adjusting for any anomaly. He trained the scope to a set of pre-programmed coordinates aimed at the Osiris Nebula and settled back to watch and listen. His scope was also equipped with a highly sensitive antenna array, located in his ample back yard. It wasn't a massive dish like those of thousands of years ago, but it was as effective with the assistance of modern technology and ultra-high-speed computing. He closed his eyes for a moment, taking in the interstellar radio signals and the ether of the cosmos. He was soon fast asleep.

Sometime later Filo woke with a start. *What was that,* he thought to himself. He'd heard something through the phones, a radio signal of some kind perhaps or maybe just a natural variance in the ether of the space he was focussed on. It did tend to waver and oscillate from time to time, so he wasn't overly surprised by the anomaly.

In all the history of the World, no-one had even located any sign of life beyond Terrania. No radio bursts, no signs of intelligent life through spectrum studies of exoplanets, nothing whatsoever. Of course, when war upon war fractured the World, astronomy ground to a halt. When society settled into its new state of being, astronomy became something of a casual pastime rather than a serious undertaking. It certainly didn't attract any form of governmental support or funding, so discoveries were rare and deep space exploration long forgotten.

Filo knew that space missions had been launched in the distant past, thousands of them to be frank. Some were deep space missions aimed at far distant objects and a few even tried interstellar travels using light sails to propel their small probes across the vastness of space between galaxies. No-one knew what became of any of those objects. For all Filo knew they were still out there, lost forever. Pity.

Filo looked at the telemetry on his quantum screen. There was indeed a spike on the data stream. He rewound the recording and listened, *zzzzzt!* There it was, a clear and significant carrier of some kind, not static. It sounded like the hash of a radio signal as the relay switch released after a broadcast. Looking at the preceding data that was recorded he could see a spectrum of some kind, a low-level source which had lasted 48 secs. Filo did some calculations to try and home in on the source. He was quite experienced having traced many signals from pulsars and quasars and knew how to find what he was looking for. When the computer spat out the results he was puzzled. The information made no sense. He ran the calculations again and got the exact same result, *how could this be?* It was too strong to be a celestial signal which meant it was close.

As silly as it felt to him, he turned his attention to the optical telescope and looked at the exact point of the signal, expecting to see a distant object that might explain the signal, something undiscovered perhaps. Almost immediately he spied a glint of light. He drew his eye away from the lens and wiped it with the back of his hand then looked again. A moment or two later there was another glint, then two more. *What?* The glints appeared to be from high orbiting objects. Filo knew this was impossible as all the old satellites had burnt up long ago and nothing was up there anymore. The technology of today dispensed with the need for satellites in any case, so what was he seeing?

Filo followed protocol, reached for his communicator and called his friend and fellow astronomer Jako, "I need confirmation. Can you see it?"

"Yes," replied Jako, "Glints of light in high orbit, but that's impossible."

"I know, but we both see it. What do we do now?"

"Take hi res pictures, record as much data as you can for as long as you can and bring it to the society tomorrow. Can you get away from work?"

"That shouldn't be a problem," Filo said thinking of the mindless rotes he spent watching the automated systems that never needed him to intervene.

"Right then, be at the society at 10 rotations. Someone might know what it is."

Filo noted the time in his electronic diary, a tool he lived by. As discussed, he recorded everything, the vision and sounds, for the next 2 rotes and then it stopped as suddenly as it started. He still had no idea what he'd witnessed. He collated the data onto a pocket drive and went inside. In the bedroom his wife and children slept, breathing deeply and undisturbed by his presence. He joined them and, after a while drifted off himself.

At dawn, just after 7 rotes he woke. His family were already eating, and he joined them feeling somewhat excited to share his discovery, whatever it was.

"How was your night Filo," asked Sanita after giving him a kiss on the cheek.

"Well, I may have discovered something!"

"Really father, what was it?" asked his eldest child Mika

"I don't really know."

"Oh, so does that mean it's not really a discovery?" asked Filo's daughter.

"Don't be rude Janeya," said Sanita but all the children laughed as did Filo.

"It's only a discovery when we confirm it and I'm doing that today."

"Really Filo? What about work," asked Sanita making her frustration apparent.

"I'm taking a few rotes off; this could be important."

"What do you mean, important, it's just astronomy?" she retorted.

"I saw light from a nearby source and heard what could have been radio chatter on the low-end spectrum. It's not an area that is used much on the planet, so it's strange."

"What could it be father?" asked his youngest child Kita.

"It might just be a signal bouncing off something but that wouldn't explain the glints of light. We have nothing up there anymore, but if I had to guess I would say a vessel of some kind."

"Are you sure?" asked Sanita.

"Of course not! I'm just guessing but it's too close to be a natural phenomenon. The travel time is in the mins which means it's very close. And before you ask, no, we don't have any spaceships."

"Could we have built one?" asked Janeya who was suddenly very serious,

"Possibly, but it is counter to everything we've strived for as a people. The League of Governors is not interested in space exploration and for thousands of years we've found nothing out there, so in that respect our forefathers were right to focus on more helpful things," Filo suggested.

"So, what are you suggesting Filo? It's alien?" asked Sanita looking a little concerned.

"Perhaps." Filo answered but then noticed the fear on his children's faces and thought quickly, "Or it's just a fickle signal that we will easily explain when we analyse the data. Nothing to be concerned about, I'm sure." He grimaced which only Sanita noticed.

"Well, whatever it is it's not going to make the children late for schooling. Wash up and get ready for the transport. You can't be late!" Sanita demanded.

"Yes mother," they all droned.

As soon as they were out of the room Sanita looked at Filo, "What do you really think?"

"I saw blinking lights, not reflections and different colours too, like nav lights or anti-collision lights. I'm convinced it's a ship. The carrier too, it came from the exact same source. My immediate concern is that a faction has developed this technology, but I cannot understand what would motivate such actions. We have peace and prosperity. No-one goes without."

"Oh my," said Sanita, now lost for words.

Filo continued, "However, I think there are too many reasons to suspect it's not of our own making, which means it can only be alien. I simply don't have the evidence to make any determination. Hopefully someone at the Society will."

They finished the morning meal in silence.

At 10 rotes Filo walked into the building that housed the Astronomical Society, which was more of a club than a major institution. His colleagues had assembled having been made aware of his potential discovery. Filo noticed a formal meeting had been gazetted and when everyone was seated the Lead Astronomer, Barkou called the meeting to order.

"Filo, tell us of your findings."

"Thank you Barkou but it might be simpler to have everyone witness the data first."

He took a device from his pocket and placed it on the table. It immediately tethered to the projection wall and audio system and began to play. No one spoke, all transfixed on the images and sounds. Glints of light, sounds that zipped in and out. Carrier signals on the low F band. They sat for two rotes absorbing every detail. Chatting occasionally, replaying certain sounds and scenes and then Barkou opened the topic for discussion, "Filo, your thoughts please."

"I believe we are looking at a vessel of some kind. Logic tells me it must be ours, constructed in secret but for reasons I cannot glean. Revolution seems illogical. On the other hand, given our society's stance on space exploration, it cannot be of our making and is therefore alien but given our total failure in the past to identify any other life, the theory is also doubtful. To my mind the mostly likely explanation is that we are looking at a Terranian vessel."

Filo continued, explaining his observations and theories at length. Why he believed certain probabilities over other possibilities and reasons why certain concepts were impossible.

As he spoke, those that agreed with certain statements lightly pounded the tabletop with their fists. The deniers simply held an open hand on the table. Those that had not yet taken on an opinion kept their hands in their laps. Filo concluded after about 15 mins opening the discussion to the table.

"What should we do?" came one short but succinct voice.

"I really have no idea," replied Filo.

"And if they are aliens, why bother with us?" asked another.

"Again, not something I can offer an answer to. I have asked myself the very same questions and many more."

Then one learned fellow spoke up, a professor of linguistics as it turned out, "May I listen to the audio again please?"

"Why of course Ludic. Which part?"

"It matters not."

"Very well."

Filo repeated the playback and Ludic listened intently for a few mins then raised his hand to indicate he'd heard enough."

Barkou looked upon him, "What are you thinking Ludic?"

"I believe we are hearing voices in the carrier signal."

This time the reaction was one of overwhelming astonishment.

"Please explain Ludic."

"There are various tones, squawks and annotations within the carrier. To the untrained ear they sound like crackles in the ether, but they have substance, I'm certain of it. They are all different. One will be a higher pitch than the next and there are inflections too. It's communication. They seem to be exchanging messages just as we are doing here and now. I..." Ludic hesitated.

"Please go on," suggested Barkou.

Ludic was careful not to undermine the provider of the data, "As Filo has suggested, I don't believe they are of this World. They are not Terranian."

The astronomers debated for many mins when someone finally said, "We need to report this."

"Indeed, we do," confirmed Barkou, "I suggest we send a delegation to the capital and present Filo's findings. Filo, you will go with Ludic and me. The three of us will present the evidence and allow the governors to decide what it is and what to do about it."

The group agreed.

Chapter 3 – The Governors

Genova was the centre of government for the entire planet. It housed the League of Governors, 25 in all representing 24 times zones with an alternate appointed so there could never be a tied vote in keeping with the planetary constitution. No-one could abstain from a vote, so a result was always achieved. The Governors each spent one lunar cycle in the city and one lunar cycle at their home province. The system was simple. It didn't really need to be complicated. The planet was enjoying a harmonic existence with a like-minded approach to the good of the environment and the people. Decisions were rarely heavily debated because the constitution set standards that guided the decision-making process.

In the year 13839 an environmental decision came to the League of Governors. They faced a dilemma over a dam, one that had existed for almost 500 years. Its purpose was to generate hydroelectric power, but it had become expensive to maintain, and alternative energy sources made it redundant. The decision was not about decommissioning the dam but whether to deconstruct it and return the region to normal. While such issues in the past would have created a firestorm of debate with the environment against commercial interests, the result was passed with almost no discussion. The constitution was clear, when the natural state of things could be renewed, it would be so. There were exceptions of course, such as flood mitigation, but in this case, it was not an issue as there were no populations downstream. So, the dam was slowly drained and deconstructed. The refuse was used elsewhere; nothing was wasted. The region was returned to its natural state over a period of 400 solar quarters, causing no disruption to habitat and wildlife. Simple, logical decisions.

The city itself was magnificent with gleaming glass and steel high rise structures as ornate as any intricate sculpture. All were self-sufficient with their own eco and recycling systems for water and waste. With planetary weather systems stable, the forefathers were able to accurately plan the locations of cities to take full advantage of rains. It wasn't a perfect process and backup systems were built into the city networks, but they were rarely needed and never for long. All vehicles were eco-friendly with most people reliant on the mass transporters that moved about on a perfectly maintained timetable. Suburbs spread out around the city centre just like they had in the past, but they were cleverly built to avoid transport congestion or overpopulation. If a suburb reached maximum capacity, it was closed to new residents and a new suburb created if required but population growth was slow and strictly maintained to guarantee no strain on resources. If the League of Governors were made aware of a population spike, constitutional controls were imposed to slow the birth rate. No-one argued with this and, yes there was disappointment, but everyone understood that the dangers of runaway population growth were far worse than having to wait to have a child. Every decision was designed to maintain planetary balance.

As this was a sitting cycle for the league, Barkou, Filo and Ludic wasted no time arranging to meet with the Governors. The League's open-door policy was one that enabled all the people to meet their representatives face to face if desired and individual governors spent more time talking to constituents than sitting in the hallowed halls of the League. The trio was soon in the office of, Garon, the representative of their home province, Estonita. After the traditional pleasantries and introductions were completed Garon sat at a meeting table and invited the trio to join him. A scribe machine was engaged to keep a record of the exchange, as required under constitutional law. ALL meetings were recorded.

"Thank you for seeing us, Garon," said Barkou, "We hope you do not find this news disturbing."

"On the contrary, men of science may not have the interest of the League that they once did, but when there are discoveries to reveal, I'm a very keen listener. What have you found?"

Barkou gestured towards Filo who took the cue, "Garon, I believe there's a ship in orbit above our planet. I believe right now that it is hiding behind our Moon so we cannot see it with our telescopes or hear its signals."

"A spaceship?"

"Yes sir," Filo then played an edited version of the audible and optical data before continuing, "I detected it with a small radio telescope and then confirmed the discovery visually before it went silent and slipped out of view, but I believe it's still there," explained Filo.

"I have confirmed Filo's findings," added Ludic, "The recordings clearly indicate a craft of some kind, maybe more and we believe the audibles we caught were radio communications on the low F band. We think words were spoken, but we do not know the language."

Garon didn't realise immediately that his mouth was gaping revealing his astonishment, "My goodness, this is unprecedented."

"Well, no, it isn't," said Barkou, "Thousands of years ago space travel was common. We sent men and women to our own Moon and other planets in our system. There are probes still travelling in space that our forefathers send to study distant objects. It's only due to the ravages of war and the coming together of the people for peace and prosperity that we discarded such practices."

"I take your point which prompts the question, who are they?"

"We see only two possibilities Garon," suggested Barkou, "They are a radical group of Terranians who have secretly developed space technology and are now actively launching into space. That said, we see this as unlikely because it would be nearly impossible to hide the expenditure, not to mention a launch, unless they did so from the outer territories. Even so, how would they move something so large across vast areas of wilderness? And a ship of this size would have been constructed in space. It is too large, so multiple launches would have been required during the construction which would have taken many quarters, not to mention the lack of expertise. We simply do not have the skills to do this."

"I see your point Barkou. So, what is the other possibility?"

"They're aliens," said Filo bluntly.

Garon looked stunned, "Aliens?"

"Yes. The language we heard was unintelligible, almost indistinguishable in the ether. Also, if they have travelled here from afar, then it's likely they have superior abilities and perhaps weaponry," suggested Filo.

"What might their intentions be?" asked Garon.

"That would be purely speculative but there are only two or three possibilities. They are explorers and are here to study our planet. They are fleeing a dead world or something catastrophic and looking for somewhere new to settle or..." Filo hesitated.

"Or?"

"They're here to take possession of our world."

Garon looked horrified this time, "An invasion? Surely not."

"It's also possible that they're just passing by and stopped because they saw life here. We don't know for certain," added Barkou, "We simply wanted to make the League aware of this. What you do with the information is entirely up to you."

"Of course, yes indeed. I must report this to the Governors, and you must come with me. You must explain it. I do not possess the knowledge."

"Of course," answered Barkou.

In very little time a gathering of the Governors was arranged and their reaction to the news was also one of astonishment although one or two dismissed the claims as the ravings of a lunatic fringe. For the first time in a great many quarters, the Governors were at odds about how to deal with the discovery or the potential implications and a debate soon began which escalated into an argument fuelled by panic it seemed. It soon threatened to descend into something more undesirable.

Filo, realising that the mayhem was going to achieve nothing called out to the Governors, "Why don't we just ask them why they're here?"

The remark had an instantaneous effect and the halls fell silent.

Chapter 4 – Titania

ISS Titania was the biggest and most modern war ship of any ever constructed and the flagship of the First Andromedan Fleet. It carried a crew of 10,000 souls, all highly trained and very capable. It was an L Class vessel, a hyper cruiser measuring almost three sheps from stem to stern. It carried enough firepower to lay siege to an entire planet for several cycles and enough power and supplies to remain in a siege orbit for an extensive period, hundreds of cycles. Support vessels were unnecessary as the ship had its own armada of stealth interceptors and the capacity to carry an army of 5000 in addition to the crew, which it was doing very comfortably as it came out of hyperspace just over 50 light years from the target planet, a mere spec of light from such a distance.

Admiral Karlou Vardourn watched expectantly as Titania emerged from the wormhole after a lengthy and difficult journey, "Damage report," he barked.

"Nothing significant Admiral," came the first officer's reply.

"Good, the rest of the fleet will be coming through over the next few millies, we best make room for them."

"Yes sir," said the officer, "Bring her about, make way for the fleet."

The other officers and personnel on the bridge immediately engaged the pulse engines and slid the ship out of harm's way as the spherical opening of the wormhole continued to shimmer where the fold in space met their exit point.

Over the next several millies more ships came, battle cruisers, interceptor carriers, smaller swift destroyers, personnel carriers and assorted frigates and other military vessels. Among them were civilian ships carrying survivors of the Andromedan population.

When the last of the ships were through, the wormhole persisted for a while then evaporated. The Admiral's eyes darkened as the last glint of the sphere disappeared. His thoughts were elsewhere for a moment then he turned to the bridge crew, "Open a hailing frequency and call the ships to muster."

"Yes sir!"

The order was despatched and the ships manoeuvred into a defensive cube, all moving at pulse speed. It was like a huge, slow-motion ballet. The military ships cubed around the civilian vessels forming a protective shield. When all were settled the Admiral broadcast to the fleet,

"We have arrived at our designated coordinates safely. I am grateful for that. This was not an easy journey for many of us. Aside from the dangers of jumping space so many times, we leave behind family and friends, never to cross paths again. We seek a new World after the decimation of our own. We were fortunate to have been chosen from the billions in our planetary system, and I know for many of us, it doesn't sit easy knowing so many are already dead and I expect by now that civilisation as we knew it is no more." The Admiral paused but no-one said anything, "We were also fortunate to discover worlds like our own and more fortunate to have the technology to escape. I can tell you now that our armada was one of seven to make the jump to seek out these known worlds. I can only hope that the other six fleets have been able to succeed as we have. Alas we will never know. For now, we will secure all vessels, make repairs and prepare for our final jump to a new World. I do not know what we will find there but our spectrum analysis indicates it is a green world with oxygen, liquid water and most importantly is in the temperate zone of its system. Its days are slightly shorter than ours so it shouldn't be too much of an adjustment and the temperatures are stable, but we may find it a little on the cooler side. That is also something we will adjust to in time. One thing I know you're all wondering is whether there is life on this world. I would venture to say yes, but to what degree or intelligence we will only glean as we get closer. At this distance any radio signals would be too scattered to interpret, so the answer for now is, we do not know. We have but one more jump to make so for now I say well done and good luck."

The Admiral nodded to his First Officer, Yeovale Darnuth then said, "Make ready your ships for the final jump. We depart in 10 cycles. That is all."

Most of the vessels reported little or no damage, none that would cause a delay. Admiral Vardourn was astonished that they had suffered no losses during the journey, having completed 27 jumps to reach this point. It had taken the better part of 2000 cycles to make the journey thus far, but he knew the most difficult phase was yet to come. After the final jump, they would still be half a light year from the target planet. Even though all the ships carried near light speed technology, maintaining that speed for so long would be impossible as the ships resources would not allow it. In simple terms the longer the ships travelled at light speed, the faster they consumed fuel. The calculations that were made for the final phase suggested it would take them at least four times longer to complete their flight. Keeping an entire fleet and its population settled for such an unprecedented time-period was of great concern. Most civilians had never travelled in space, and some were already raising concerns about their conditions and the lack of room. How would they cope with another 9000 cycles of travel ahead? It couldn't be helped.

Admiral Vardourn retired to his quarters to get some rest before the final jump when his commlink buzzed, "Yes?"

"My apologies sir, it's the Supreme Leader, Bishon Grudek," The Comms Officer explained.

"Put him through."

"Yes sir"

There was a crackle on the devise and then a brief silence, "Hello Karlou, how are you feeling?"

"I am weary Bishon, what about you?"

"Much the same but we are nearly there, correct?"

"Well, it depends how you look at it. Close in distance but much farther in terms of time," suggested Karlou.

"Why can we not jump nearer to the planet?"

"There's the risk of causing a catastrophic effect if we place a wormhole too near. The gravitational wave we create at close-proximity may be destructive. We need distance to enable it to harmlessly disburse."

"I understand. You have done very well getting us this far and we remain in your hands until the arrival," suggested Bishon.

"Thank you, my old friend. We have been quite lucky I would venture to say," Karlou added.

"Not luck. We have known each other for a long time and served together in the Independence War, I know better."

"Thank you again and rest assured, when the journey is done my leadership role will be done. I was only ever going to take charge for the journey. I will then serve at your pleasure Bishon."

"I am lucky to have someone as astute as you by my side. Your skills will be most valuable to us all I think," Bishon paused then asked, "What of this planet, is it what we seek?"

"I believe so. It is uncannily similar to ours in rotation, climate and length of day. We could not have been more fortunate," said Karlou.

"What potential of inhabitants?"

"Well sir, I would never understate the possibility. We learned that the hard way did we not?" Karlou said which made his stomach squirm.

"Indeed, we did and that is why we're here. We were unprepared and unable to stop the Borche. When we realised their power, it was too late. They swept through us like a swarm. We had no choice but to hold them until we could plan an escape," Bishon explained even though Karlou was all too aware of the events that had transpired to bring them to this point.

"I am saddened that it came to this. So many now facing death and enslavement. All our planets will fall I fear," suggested Karlou.

"That is sadly true, but we have saved millions with the seven fleets. We escaped undetected and it's highly doubtful that we will see the Borche again. Their conquest exhausted them I feel and they are not equipped to chase us in seven directions over this kind of distance."

"Probably," is all that Karlou said.

"You are not so sure?"

"We've been so wrong before."

"True. So, we have 9000 cycles to contemplate our new lives after this final jump. What will be your first action?" asked Bishon.

"Once we leave hyperspace I will scan for broadcast signals from the planet. That will tell us immediately if there is intelligent life, unless they have other means of communications. Our reliance on radio technology was our undoing. We were detected and, well you know the rest. They may be more careful. Who knows? I am simply speculating of course. It may be a virgin world ready for the taking. That would be the ideal situation."

"I hope you are correct on the latter point then," added Bishon.

"We will soon know," added the Admiral.

"I have taken up enough of your time Karlou. I wish you well on the last phase of our journey. We should meet once the jump is complete, yes?"

"I would like that very much Bishon."

"Good. I'll see you on the other side."

"Very good old friend. See you soon." Karlou said as he cut of the comm link.

With that Admiral Vardourn caught a sleep cycle, enough to revive him from his fatigue. Sleep had not come easily in recent times. Cataclysmic war tends to have that effect.

He returned to the bridge a few moments before the jump. He need not have been there for the preparations. His people were well versed in the procedure and highly able. His job was simply to give the order.

He sat in his spacious chair and once again watched as the neutron charge was launched several hundred sheps ahead of the fleet. Once in place it would erupt like a mini supernova, crossing the threshold of space and time simultaneously then a second projectile would be fired into the void quite literally punching a hole through the fabric of space. The void or wormhole would, in theory, remain stable long enough time for the entire fleet to pass through, covering 49.5 light years in an instant, ironically their shortest jump to date. The danger was some unseen force within the time spectrum that might disturb the wormhole and cause it to collapse prematurely. It hadn't happened yet but even a flawless jump puts strains on the ships, and many had reported superficial damage after one jump or another. Mathematically they should have lost several ships by now, but the scientists and astronomers had done good work and allowed the fleet to avoid any trouble.

The haste that was required to enable the six fleets to escape left no time for testing. They simply had to rely on the technicians, mathematicians and astronomers to get it right. The jump process was unprecedented in Andromedan history, so having a perfect succession of jumps over many parsecs to this point was indeed a miracle.

One more jump thought Vardourn just as the wormhole opened. All was in readiness. His ship, the Titania would lead as always, and then each ship would follow in a designated order, military then civilian, then military and so on. The Supreme Leader would come through on the third ship, the ISS Vittorius, a Supreme Class Battle Cruiser, a fine ship, much decorated for its service during the hostilities with the Borche. Her captain, Cion Zanaeus was very experienced and an excellent tactician. He was the right choice to carry the Supreme Leader. Heads of State and Military Commanders were always separated in situations like this, to ensure continuity of command should disaster strike one or more ships. Only Titania was without civilians as it took the most risk with every jump it executed. The neutron charges it carried were volatile, so civilians were kept away.

The Titania edged forward and then the command was given, "Execute!" She accelerated to light speed almost instantaneously. Light speed was necessary to make the jump, any slower and the odds of a catastrophic failure increased significantly. The ship reached light speed in 0.87 of a millie. She punched into the void and at that instant the Titania rocked like something huge had hit her. Nonetheless she emerged at the designated point in a handful of micras and immediately decelerated to pulse speed. The Titania vibrated horribly and felt like she was about to come apart.

"Damage report!" demanded the Admiral.

"Coming now sir! We have fractures along sectors 9, 10 and 11 aft from decks 19 through 27. Total loss of atmosphere sir. Number 4 engine is non-compliant."

"Seal off the decks, shut down number 4; maintain pressure in all other compartments. What hit us number 1?"

"No idea sir. It's probably many light years behind us now."

"Bring her about, I have to see if the wormhole is stable."

"Yes sir."

As the ship came about Vardourn saw the wormhole, it appeared intact, "Can we get a reading Number 1?"

"Yes sir, the wormhole is weakening."

"How long have we got?"

"Hard to say sir, possibly a micra, perhaps much less."

Vardourn clenched a fist, "Would they be aware of the problem?"

"Not if they're preparing to jump, all power would be channelled to the light engines sir."

"So, they could be inside when it collapses?"

"Yes admiral."

"What happens then?"

"No-one knows sir; it's never happened before."

The Admiral looked around the bridge, "Does anyone know what might happen?"

"Um, yes sir," It was a young cadet, barely old enough to have a uniform.

The admiral looked at her and instinctively thought she was probably a dignitary's child who was given special treatment but shook off the idea immediately, "Give me your thoughts."

"There are several possibilities sir, they could simply emerge at a point between the beginning of the jump and here, many light years from us. They could be evaporated by the destruction of the vortex; they might even be thrust into another dimension. It's untested science sir," explained the cadet.

"Your best guess cadet?"

The young female gulped, clearly feeling the pressure, she was now under, "Well sir, we created the power of a neutron star and then punched into it, that's an awful lot of power, which we have allowed to simply dissipate naturally after our previous jumps. A collapse would, in my opinion, cause a tear in the space time continuum and any ship within the vortex at that moment would be pulverised sir, turned to dust."

"And are we talking the loss of one ship or many?"

"Well, the journey to us is fractional time wise but in real terms there could be twenty ships or more in the vortex even though we go in one at a time. The space and time we know doesn't exist in the vortex, so even though we're in and out in an instant, we're crossing a distance that can only be measured in millions of sheps. Theoretically we could all be in there at the same time."

Vardourn considered the explanation, "Thank you cadet. I hope you are wrong."

"Ship emerging sir!" called the chief observer.

It was the super heavy civilian cruiser, DSS Siansus. She carried 70,000 souls and she came through unscathed it seemed.

"Check their status!"

"The Comms Officer sent a radio burst to the Siansus. She reported that she was suffering nothing more than a few burnt power units in the light engines.

Vardourn didn't feel relieved, there were still 78 ships carrying five million travellers yet to make it through.

"Sir, the Vittorius is emerging."

The Admiral watched and was thinking of his good friend Bishon being safe when a huge flash blinded him for an instant. It was quickly followed by a surge of energy that swept the Titania like a wave hitting a splinter. They were suddenly swept along at an astonishing velocity and tumbling uncontrollably. Many of the crew who weren't strapped in we flung about hitting bulkheads, computers, controls and other equipment. Warning bells clanged and emergency lights flashed. In the confusion Vardourn barked out an order, "Fire the emergency dampeners!"

The First Officer, strapped into his flight seat, was fighting the G forces and struggled to reach the control desk but managed to flip the cover off the emergency control. He hammered a large button with his fist which immediately engaged the dampeners. The ship was still writhing and rolling but the computers were able to fire a series of retro bursts to dampen the effect. In a short time, the Titania was stable but still travelling at an incredible speed.

"Damage report!" called Vardourn.

"No telemetry yet sir."

"Get the engines and power units back online. Do we have emergency life support?"

"Yes sir. We have 12 cycles worth of air."

"So, we have 12 cycles to get the ship operational. See to it Number 1!"

"Yes sir."

Then the Admiral called out, "Do we have Nav computers?"

"Rebooting sir."

"Then don't waste time talking to me. Report when you know something."

"Yes sir."

The entire crew respected Admiral Vardourn. He was a great leader militarily and had served with distinction, that was true, but he was also resourceful and intelligent. He had survived many catastrophic situations that would have seen most others fail and die. He was always calm under pressure. He was also fair. He expected nothing short of excellence but unlike many of the Andromedan Fleet commanders, he refused to be ruthless. It was the way of their culture, but he felt it better to unleash that venom on the enemy and not his own people. It had the desired effect. He enjoyed unwavering support and excellence from his officers and crew. He looked at the external viewing screen and noticed the stars and galaxies were blowing by so fast they appeared to be stretching, which didn't make any sense.

The Nav Officer made her report, "Sir, we've have been swept billions of sheps away from the wormhole. I have no contact with Vittorius or Siansus and there's no sign of the rest of the fleet. I put our position," the Comms officer hesitated, "This can't be right?"

"What is it?

"Sir, the Nav Computer is suggesting we're only 500,000 sheps from the new planet."

"What? Is that possible?"

No-one answered until the Admiral turned to the cadet, "What say you?"

"Um, well sir, yes. I believe we were struck by the gravitational wave created by the collapse of the vortex and driven along by the explosive effect; an uncontrolled time slip I suspect. It's all theoretical of course but it would explain our acceleration."

"I see. So, the Vittorius and Siansus?"

"The Siansus is probably suffering the same effect as us. They don't have the dampening capabilities that we do, so they will struggle to overcome the effect and may tumble infinitely longer, sir."

And the Vittorius?"

The cadet looked nervous but answered the Admiral without hesitation, "I would anticipate a total loss sir unless she was clear of the vortex before it collapsed. The rest of the fleet could be scattered, or they too could be lost. We may never know. It's possible that they are hundreds of thousands of light years away."

"Could they make another jump and re-join us?"

"Doubtful sir, the Vittorius was the only other ship that could create a vortex. She was the only backup we had which is why she had to come through early. It was a safety measure."

"I see. In hindsight it may have been better to have her come through last."

"I agree sir," continued the cadet, "The other ships will be stranded in deep space and incapable of reaching us before exhausting their resources. I'm afraid, if they survived the collapse, they are doomed anyway, sir."

Admiral Karlou Vardourn felt his stomach sink and his hands shook as his body and mind processed the news, "Thank you cadet." He looked around the bridge, all eyes were on him, "Scan for our fleet. I know we are close to the planet, but we must break radio silence. We must find them."

The cadet made an expression which the Admiral noticed, "I know cadet. It's a waste of effort but what else can we do? We must try." He then turned to the Comms Officer, "Send a series of fast radio bursts and light pulse signals. Try anything you think will work to find our fleet."

"Yes sir."

Just then an engineer appeared on the bridge. He stopped and saluted the Admiral with a clenched fist hitting his chest.

"What is it?" ordered Vardourn.

"Sir, I am sorry to report that the breach in our hull caused a cascade of failures, and we lost the bulkheads in the entire aft section of the ship. All hands in the accom section are lost sir as are the engineers tending to the light engines. The main thrusters are all offline."

It was not their custom, but the gasps of horror and anguish from everyone on deck were understandable given the circumstances.

The Admiral knew that those losses were at least 3000 personnel, "Are we going to lose the ship?"

"She is severely fractured but built to hold under normal pressure...but at this speed..."

"How many people do you have?"

"Barely enough."

"Very well, do what you can to slow us down."

"Yes sir. We will have to try and activate them remotely from the midship controls; we can't get back to the main engine room in time," suggested the engineer.

"Understood," Vardourn thought for a moment, "Helm?"

"Yes sir?"

"Do you have attitude control?"

"Yes sir, we have pulse motors and secondary thrusters."

"Good, work with the remaining engineers and get us back online as soon as you can, we have to reduce speed and very soon."

"Yes sir."

As the cycles passed concerns grew. Life support wasn't yet back, and the engineers were taking too long. The scans, radio bursts and light signals had failed to detect any ships, not that anything was expected. In real terms any signal they sent might take eons to reach the fleet. Things were getting desperate when suddenly the comms opened on the bridge, it was the engineer, "Admiral, we have two of the main engines back up, turn her against the flow and fire them up. We'll use a significant amount of our fuel resources I suspect but we should be able to slow down enough."

"You heard him, turn her about and fire the engines until we're out of the wave," ordered Vardourn.

The helmsman brought the Titania about slowly. It was hard work against the gravitational effect of the wave, but he soon had her front on to the invisible flow. He hit the comm button and broadcast to the entire ship, "Brace for immediate decel," and waited a few millies then fired engines one and three at full power. The Titania shuddered horribly and everyone thought she might just crack in two. The decel effect was immediate though and loose objects all over the ship shifted in one big mass smashing into crew, fittings and bulkheads. Under normal circumstances none of these things would have been a problem but the ship was fighting a huge amount of velocity and slowing down now created new problems. A huge storage container broke loose in cargo bay 12. It contained spare parts for the jump drive and when it hit the bulkhead, every component inside was shattered or bent up. In the mess an oven broke off its footings and slid through the number 7 mess hall obliterating everything in its path including many crews who were holding on for dear life to the mess hall tables. The casualty count was rising fast. Similar incidents were happening all over the ship. Stealth Interceptors that hadn't been properly secured slid into those that were and all destroyed setting off a series of fuel fires. In hangar 17 a munitions cradle simply flew from one end of the facility to the other, hitting the bulkhead and exploding and blowing a hole in the ship which caused an immediate decompression in the entire hangar. Before the safety doors could close, 28 crew were sucked into space along with vital maintenance equipment.

Despite the problems, the engines were doing the job and the Titania was slowing. It took half a cycle and all anyone could do was hold tight and hope for the best and ultimately, they were rewarded. There was a sudden feeling of release as the ship broke through the back of the gravitational way into clear space and Titania instantly felt stable. Normal conditions were restored and the helmsman reported, "Admiral, we have control!"

"Well done everyone," announced Vardourn on the ship wide network, "I need casualty reports and damage reports as soon as you can. All hands that are able, assist with the injured. Secure the working parts of the ship. Seal all breaches, we can't afford to lose more atmosphere."

For the next few cycles everyone who could, worked on the various problems and soon most of the major issues were overcome, artificial gravity was restored, then life support. It was thought there was enough fuel in the engines to get her underway again and the engineer was confident they could maintain flight and attitude control."

"Navigation, where are we?"

"Sir we've literally been blown into the gravitational pull of the target planet."

Surprised as he was, he didn't have time to dwell and sent a message to the crew with immediate effect, "Shut down all radio comms and maintain radio silence."

The crew immediately complied.

"Helm, are we exposed?"

"Yes sir."

"OK, take up behind their moon, just in case the planet is technologically capable. I don't want our backsides swinging in the breeze," The Admiral wasn't known for such language but under the circumstances, "Number 1, we need time to assess the injuries and damage, then we can look at the planet and see what's down there. In the meantime, continue scanning for other ships."

"Sir!"

Vardourn saw the cadet shake her head, normally a class 1 offense but he let it slide. He knew she was right; it was a waste of time. They were, for now, very much alone.

The helmsman started Titania on a course to ease the vessel behind the Moon which would have two effects. It would screen them from visual detection and block any signals from their scanners, but they couldn't stay there forever, but it would provide a reasonable haven while they made repairs, if they could.

Just before the ship took shelter the Admiral glanced at the planet. It was indeed beautiful, a mixture of white, blue and green/brown. He could make out cloud formations, liquid oceans and terrain with forests, deserts and rivers and for a fleeting moment as he looked at the shadow of night, he thought he saw lights. Titania was suddenly cut off from the view and hidden behind the moon but those lights worried Admiral Karlou Vardourn. If there were lights, then there was intelligent life and technology. They may well have jumped from one conflict only to face another and they were ill equipped for a large-scale fight, but it might be their only way of surviving, so fight they would.

The Admiral looked around and noticed the cadet. She too had seen the planet. She suddenly noticed him staring at her and made an expression that he easily interpreted; she was scared.

Chapter 5 – In hiding

Admiral Vardourn inspected the damage to his ship. The fracturing along the hull in the aft sections was significant and he realised that anyone on those decks would have had no hope of getting into their survival suits nor the life pods. As he piloted a shuttle close to the exterior of the vessel, the hole in the side where the munitions had exploded proved to be catastrophically huge and would take a significant effort and much time to repair. He was convinced that he could have flown right through it. The good news was that the damage was indeed repairable and that the Titania could probably be restored to almost full function, but with a severely depleted crew. Between the accom and engineering sections, the losses had been tallied at 5291, around one third of the cruiser's military personnel, including most of the army they carried in case they needed to take the planet by force. With the other ships in the fleet, they would have had a force of 200,000 but now they had nothing. A scattering of survivors from the marine corps were rallied, barely a skeleton force. It displeased Vardourn greatly but there was little he could do.

His mind drifted back to the planet, currently out of view while they remained shielded on the far side of the moon. He had no idea what kind of beings were down there or if they might prove hostile. If so, this might be a very short stay indeed. The problem with having to move on was not a minor one because they simply had nowhere else to go. This was their one and only reachable destination. The other six fleets went in directions that at least doubled the distance they had travelled, and they did not have the resourced to make fifty or so jumps and the likelihood was that they would have had a catastrophic failure at some stage. It was simply impossible. He did wonder if, when the Titania was fully operational again, it might be able to mount a search and rescue mission back to their last jump point and perhaps the one before that but then he realised, with Vittorius almost certainly destroyed, they would have only one ship with jump capacity and if Titania failed just once their entire mission would be over. Right now, they had approximately ten thousand able bodied souls ready to deploy and that would just have to be enough to resettle. He would have to discuss this with his officers as there were no civilians of note on the flagship, another oversight he thought. At least there was one positive, all on board were trained in combat. That was reassuring.

He decided to slip the shuttle away from Titania and do a recon of the moon and perhaps take a quick look at the planet again. His shuttle was small and it was unlikely to be seen. At present they were on the night side of the planet, but this moon was far enough out to be taking some direct starlight. It was in waning gibbous which gave him only a small area of darkness within which to navigate. He would most certainly have to turn off the nav lights and dim the cockpit displays so he would be as invisible as possible. The shuttle had no stealth ability so he knew there was a remote chance someone or something might spot a tiny spec of light, but he felt it worth the risk.

Admiral Vardourn manoeuvred the shuttle closer to the moon's surface and hugged the terrain. It was a grey, lifeless and baron place. It was clearly unliveable, pockmarked with craters of all sizes, but then there were open plains that only showed signs of a few meteorite strikes here and there. In the distance appeared a mountain range but his altitude was such that he would clear it without concern. As he did, he fell out of sight of the Titania. He accelerated and watched as the ground below cascaded past. For a quarter of a cycle or so he maintained his heading until a blue crescent appear before him. He slowed and drifted a while making sure he remained in shadow. The blue crescent was the planet's atmosphere illuminated by the medium sized star that this planet was orbiting. As he pressed on the planet proper came into view as a dark void blocking out the stars, galaxies and constellations of this uncharted piece of the Universe. He drew the shuttle to a slow drift and blacked out the cockpit so he could get a better view of the scene. As he did so, he again saw lights beaming out from the planet's surface. He could see that there were cities ringing what he assumed were the equatorial sections of the globe. As he looked to the poles the lighting thinned out until there were none, but he could make out a significant iced region and thought the area uninhabitable. It would make sense that those living here would stay within the warmer zones. He looked at the cities and noticed a red hue. He wondered about it and considered that it was done by design to enhance sleep. If that was the case, then these people were truly advanced. Whether or not they were as advanced as the Andromedans, he could not tell. He could see that many of the cities were linked by vast avenues of light, transport systems perhaps. In some cases, the lighting was so concentrated he could make out coastlines and the shapes of the continents. Some of the land masses were huge indeed. Vardourn wondered how many beings occupied this world, far too many to overcome by force he thought.

Admiral Vardourn then had a thought. He re-tuned the shuttle radio, scanning the known frequencies to see if it locked into anything and sure enough it did. Immediately he could hear what must have been music. He hit the recorder and listened as the tones of the tune leaked into the cockpit. It was hard to know exactly what he was hearing but he could make out the individual tones of various instruments, droning sounds and sharper spikes and something else he couldn't quite identify but then it struck him, it was a voice. Someone or something was singing. He felt his heart miss a beat. This was unexpected and yet utterly delightful. Music! Rarely in his experience did music mean anything bad. This could be a hopeful sign.

He lost track of time as he absorbed the sweet sounds and didn't realise that he had continued to drift slowly across the moon's surface, sliding too far and instantly being hit by a full blast of the light from the parent star. It nearly blinded him and he swore to himself about being so careless. No doubt his little craft will be reflecting the light and anything focussed on the moon from the planet's surface with a telescope may well see the glint of his ship. He fired up the boosters and made a swift tight turn, back into the shadow. He realised that his burners too might be visible, but his stupidity made the situation unavoidable. Vardourn scolded himself. He was too experienced to make a rookie error like that but how could anyone not be mesmerised by such a beautiful sight. He powered on and went back to Titania.

Back on board the Admiral gathered his officers and played back what he heard, "What say you?" he asked them.

Yeovale Darnuth, the First Officer was first to speak, "It's music, I'm certain of that."

"I agree, but listen carefully, can you hear anything else?"

The recording played for a few moments as the officers pondered, then Maneva Gantu, the ship's doctor lit up with excitement. They all looked at her expectantly, "There's a voice. It is singing, is it not?"

"Yes, I think that's exactly what we can hear," said Vardourn, "I would like this run through our translator. I'm hopeful this voice will provide a baseline for us, and we can then monitor their radio signals. We need to learn as much as we can about these, beings. Perhaps look for visual carriers too."

"I will see to it sir," suggested Darnuth.

"Very good, now, look at the images I recorded. You can see there is a significant population over a large area of the planet's surface. If we can study these, we may be able to learn more about the way they live. Being high resolution images, we should be able to learn much," suggested the

Admiral as he handed the data block to Darnuth, "I want a report as soon as you are able."

"Yes Admiral," said the First Officer. He took possession of the data files and excused himself.

"Now, can someone give me a casualty report, how many injured, how many dying, how many walking wounded? Do we have enough medical supplies?"

The ships doctor made her report, and it was as bad as the Admiral expected. Medical personnel were stretched to the limit and supplies were already depleted in some cases. He then asked the engineer for a timeline on repairs and the answer was just as grim. Lack of personnel along with a lack of resources would hamper their efforts significantly.

"Can we gather what we need from this moon or the planet itself perhaps? And are we able to convert those resources into useable materials?" asked the Admiral. The consensus was, maybe, "In that case, I would suggest a recon mission initially, using stealth interceptors. They will be much less detectable to any early warning systems."

Chief of the Watch Narrom Gish agreed, "However Admiral, might I suggest we study the materials you have supplied before mustering for a flight. It will give us useful target points and perhaps enable us to avoid military installations and defensive positions."

"Agreed, see to it Chief." The Admiral paused briefly, "I want to visit the injured if I may doctor, will you accompany me?"

"Of course, Admiral, I'm going to the trauma section now if you have time?"

"Indeed, I'm eager to see how the crew is feeling," he looked at his number 2, a young but capable officer, "You have the Bridge Aarok."

"Yes sir!"

As they strolled through the corridors of the Titania, Karlou Vardourn and Maneva Gantu chatted about the events of the last several cycles. They agreed their situation was perilous and that their only option was to find a way to occupy this new world. Without an army, that might be impossible but perhaps a negotiated peace could be struck, a cap in hand approach seeking refuge. It was certainly not the nature of the Andromedan people to do such a thing. In the past everything was gained by force or fought off depending on the circumstances. Their history was filled with conflict and conquest, but they had been bested by a superior foe and forced to flee. They were not on their own planet now and should an attack be necessary to gain a foothold they may well be repulsed and what then?

"It is good that you are in charge Karlou, we need a more arbitrary approach to this situation. If Captain Vinaal or Captain Gothan were in this situation, well I don't need to tell you what they would be thinking," suggested Maneva.

Karlou and Maneva had known each other for a very long time. They met at the military academy and been colleagues on many vessels. Neither had ever take on a commitment partner, dedicating their lives instead to the Corps although their fondness for one another was evident.

"Thank you for saying so Maneva, I do feel we are in a very tight position and diplomacy may well be the only option for us. I suppose we will only know after we reconnoitre the planet."

"Agreed. Those images and the music do suggest they are well developed and perhaps, peaceful in nature but who knows how they might feel about a military vessel in their midst," Maneva suggested.

As they walked the Admiral looked at his personnel. Despite the adversity, discipline was still strong and each crew member stood to attention and saluted as he passed. He acknowledged every one of them.

"They adore you Karlou," suggested Maneva.

The Admiral blushed, "I adore them. They are brave and unwavering in their loyalty."

"That's because of you, how you treat them. You are respectful and not cruel or barbaric. How it is we managed to create a culture of fear I do not know but you were a beacon in our darkest days."

"Thank you Maneva, but even our cultural choices were no match for The Borche. How do you defeat an enemy that has no honour? They killed our children and babies without blinking. It was a ruthlessness that even we could not have sunk to. In the end they were just too evil to defeat."

"Maybe we simply got an overdose of our own medicine. We were so busy fighting amongst ourselves over silly things and not paying attention to what really mattered," added Maneva.

"You are right and now; we may well have to exact the same thing on these unsuspecting people. I hope not," said Karlou.

Maneva was not at all surprised by his desire to avoid a military solution, "I too hope not."

They arrived at the infirmary where the Admiral met with the many injured. The majority were suffering from fractures and abrasions due to being thrown about while tumbling in the gravity wave. Some of the injuries were horrendous. Despite the obvious pain being suffered by so many, there was hardly a sound that would indicate their pain. They were trained to accept it; to overcome adversity and here they were demonstrating those traits before their Admiral.

"You have made me so very proud. You are a credit to the Corps. I wish you a speedy recovery. I need you back to your best very soon. Thank you for your service and let us not forget those who have made the ultimate sacrifice. They died with honour.

"Hoorah!" came the unanimous reply.

"Hoorah," answered the Admiral and he saluted the group with his four fingers open across his chest, a gesture of understanding in the Corps. Then he turned to Maneva, "I must get back to the Bridge. If you need anything, please let me know."

"You are very kind Karlou, but I know that there's nothing you can do for us; our supplies cannot be replenished."

He smiled and held her gaze for a moment, "Perhaps we can find something on the planet."

"Perhaps. I wish you luck."

"Thank you," and he left, returning to the Bridge.

It was several cycles before First Officer Yeovale Darnuth returned after analysing the materials supplied by the Admiral's impromptu look at the planet. There was good news to report, "Sir we have magnified your images and scanned everything using quantum algorithms," Darnuth pressed the data block and the images appeared on a multiplex of screens, "These are cities," he said pointing at large light clusters, "We count over 100 cities in multiple continents, most straddling the equatorial regions. Many are interconnected with large transport corridors, and shipping channels. The land transportation appears to be communal, large train like machines. We see very few individual vehicles."

"Interesting. Does that mean anything do you think?" asked the Admiral.

"It may mean nothing or they have a totally different approach to moving about compared to us. They may have a hive mentality. It's hard to tell from pictures but there is one striking discovery admiral," Darnuth paused for effect.

"And what is that Yeovale," asked the Admiral. The other officers were a little surprised by the informality of using a first name.

"There appears to be no military existence, at all. We cannot see any sign of installations, launch pads, defensive structures, armies or air bases. Nothing," reported Darnuth.

"Nothing?"

"Nothing sir!"

"Could they be hidden or underground?" asked the Admiral.

"I suppose it's possible sir, but I suspect not. Another point that is clear is they do not appear to have any satellites systems, or any capacity to launch into space. Your data covers their sky on this side of the planet from hemisphere to hemisphere and we cannot see anything in orbit. Not a single thing."

"Is that so? I never thought to look while I was out there. Fascinating. That could mean they are not too advanced could it not?"

"Possibly or they have simply evolved without the desire to explore. We cannot know for certain, until we meet them," added Darnuth.

The Admiral paused, then turned to his officers, "We must mount a recon mission immediately. We are low on medical supplies and repair materials. We must get to the surface. Please arrange it Number 1."

"Yes sir!"

"And Yeovale? You are not to be detected under any circumstances, understood?"

"Of course, sir!"

"And assume they're hostile! Take weapons, stealth suits, oh and respirators, we don't know the atmosphere fully yet, our analysers are offline."

"Sir, yes sir!"

The Admiral looked at the viewing screens again and absorbed the images of their new home and wondered about the people; could they live in peace together? He certainly hoped so.

Chapter 6 – Contact

Filo returned home from Genova after meeting with the League of Governors. His suggestion, to contact the vessel or vessels beyond the Moon was discussed and accepted. Given that he and his colleagues were the best qualified to deal with an astronomical problem such as this, they were charged with the responsibility of making first contact on behalf of the League. In this society, governance didn't necessarily mean taking control of a situation and given the extraordinary circumstances, no-one really knew what was right or wrong. Astronomers it seemed were the right fit for an alien contact and most likely to be seen as a lesser threat than someone of a perceived higher standing. In the end it was simply guesswork.

A message had been formulated, recorded and would be transmitted on a loop while the Astronomical Society listened for a response. Rosters were set and each member allocated slots within which they would monitor the F band for any incoming signal.

With the help of Jako, they set up Filo's antenna array and programmed a transmitter to relay the message on rotating F band frequencies at times when the Moon was able to be targetted, which varied constantly. When out of line of sight sending a signal was impossible as there were simply no satellite relays in existence anymore. Given the circumstances it was thought that this kind of approach was adequate so whenever the Moon was visible to Filo and his team, they would transmit and monitor for any response. No-one was sure if the message would even be heard and if it were, would it be understood by the aliens. Time would tell.

Filo and Jako, uploaded the message to the transmitter drive and as the Moon rose above the horizon, they pressed the transmit button and the message began to beam out...

"We are the people of Terrania, and we welcome you to our World. We are people of peace and cooperation and would hope to open a dialogue with you to learn of your reasons for visiting our planet. The League of Governors invite you to make contact by responding to this message on this frequency. We look forward to your response. Peace be with you."

It was a simple message, one that was considered non-aggressive and straight to the point. Who are you and what do you want was the basic tone. No need to mince words. They could have listed a series of questions but that could be dealt with later, if indeed any reply came. For now, attempting contact was all that the Governors considered necessary. If nothing came of it, life would go on, maybe.

There were some who thought that making contact might be inviting trouble but if indeed their intentions were hostile, a simple welcome message might be enough to curtail any ill intent.

Filo was excited and turned to Jako, "Now we wait."

"Indeed, we do. I'm going home to rest. I'll take over from you in the next quarter."

With that Jako left and Filo got comfortable in his favourite chair, headset on. He listened as the Quantum program did its job, sending the signal across the F band spectrum, tracking the Moon, and listening for a response. How long might it take he wondered, it could be a very long time. First, they had to come out from behind the Moon and second, they had to be listening. Success was totally reliant on luck it seemed.

On board Titania, a handpicked crew was boarding one of the undamaged Stealth Interceptors. They had been charged with making their way to the surface, their primary mission to identify possible supplies to enable repairs to Titania and the other damaged interceptors, shuttles and equipment. Given the lack of information about materials available, any repair work would probably require improvisation. Their secondary mission was to reconnoitre the target area and learn anything they could of the people inhabiting the planet and to identify potential food and water sources. They were, under no circumstances, to make contact or engage with the indigenous life. Landing on the planet may be perceived as hostile so they would avoid the cities and approach the more isolated plains that had been photographed. The marines would wear sealed stealth suits and respirators to avoid detection and potential pathogens. There was no telling what diseases might exist here and every effort would be made to avoid contamination. Anything brought back on the suits back would be sanitised accordingly through ultraviolet filters.

Chief of the Watch, Narrom Gish reported to Admiral Vardourn, "All is ready sir."

"Very well, let's not stand on ceremony, send them now."

"Yes sir," Gish tapped his communicator, "You have a go!"

The bridge personnel watched as a Stealth Interceptor eased its way through the docking. Once clear of the Titania, it engaged a cloak, making it virtually invisible to the naked eye. Its radio signals would, of course, still be detectable but they were ordered to always maintain strict radio silence. The only indication that the interceptor existed was a slight ripple in the visual line between the viewer and the surface of the Moon but if you didn't know there was a ship in front of you, you would barely see it and probably write it off as some kind of mirage. It was amazing technology but not enough to trick The Borche. Now everyone was hoping the people of this planet were not as well equipped and the stealth technology would be adequate. Studying the photographs taken by Admiral Vardourn certainly suggested that these people had little in the way of significant space communications, radar systems, any form of military presence or anything beyond terrestrial radio. It was ripe for the taking, should that become a necessity, but the Admiral was hoping that would not be necessary.

The Stealth Interceptor wasn't designed to carry a lot of personnel; it was a fighter, so it had been stripped down to make room for a small contingent. Between the pilot and co-pilot, there was still room for the half dozen marines. It wasn't comfortable but they weren't going to be crammed in the machine for long. Some space was left for stowing anything of value, but this was essentially a fact-finding mission. They cleared the Titania and followed the curvature of the Moon before emerging planet side. Their landing site had been determined after studying the Admiral's data as the most likely place to provide the resources they needed, and the coordinates locked into the nav-computer. An entire program had to be written so the computers knew what to interpret; the photographs proved very helpful in that regard and the quantum program quickly rendered a surface schematic and navigational coordinates. Several other landing sites had been chosen should their primary target not prove optimal.

The Interceptor descended and soon approached the atmosphere. They would descend into the daylight zone to reduce any chance of being spotted by the naked eye during entry; however, the ship was coated in a substance that enabled a seamless insertion into the planet's atmosphere without any heat trace or smoke trail, and it worked perfectly here. The pilot, Arda Guz was now free flying the craft, gliding it at high speed to the designated landing zone. Only, when necessary, would she engage thrusters to land. For now, she was trying hard to avoid any sonic effects, however, the initial insertion into the atmosphere made that unavoidable, which is why they cut through the atmospheric membrane well to the north where it appeared no-one lived. The sonic boom would simply dissipate and go unnoticed. From there a rapid, high-altitude sortie to near the inhabited zone would be required and then the tricky air-braking manoeuvres to the landing zone. It all went very well.

During the descent Arda was able to take in the scenery. Initially she saw great sheets of ice then dry ground, oceans, rivers, mountain ranges with white peaks, green valleys, forests and vast grasslands. As she moved towards the equatorial regions she began a series of s-bend movements to slow the craft down. The area identified for landing was behind a series of steep hills which should buffer any noise made by the landing boosters and hopefully, if heard, would be put down to a rock fall or distant thunder. As they approached, Arda and her co-pilot scanned for life forms. Nothing significant was detected. The craft was now descending in a fast glide aimed directly at a gorge behind the hills. Arda pulled up the nose to the point of a stall to slow the craft even more and just as the warnings chimed, she levelled off. They were now only a few hundred spans from the surface and as soon as the Interceptor fell below the crest of the hill she fired the boosters. In a few millies the craft gently touched down in a clearing beside a creek, shrouded by a copse of trees. Even so, stealth mode would remain active to avoid any chance of visual detection. The only way anyone or anything would find them would be to literally run into the ship.

As they shut down the engines, the marines did final checks on their suits and equipment. They would carry weapons yes but were ordered not to engage and to use only stun mode if they had to shoot. Stealth suits were strange and made simple tasks much more difficult. Being technically invisible meant a marine had to do most things by feel, including the use of weaponry. They'd all been trained and practiced endlessly so that it became instinctive, and they chose only side arms in this instance to enable easier movement. They could already feel the difference in gravity, which wasn't too much compared to home, another good sign. When all was ready, Arda punched the cargo door release, and it slid away on the left side of the craft revealing for the first time a close-up view of the planet at ground level. It was magically beautiful, untainted and serene and all six of the marines just stared for a moment before regaining their senses. The squad leader jumped to the ground, a sandy loam-like surface with scattered pebbles and rocks amongst tufts of grass, no doubt a creation of the nearby creek over perhaps many eons. The ground looked easy to negotiate and when all six were of terra firma they began to walk. Initially they felt a little unsteady; in this gravity they felt lighter and their centres of gravity were slightly off, but they adjusted quickly, albeit after a few stumbles.

Using a pre-planned route that had been programmed into their heads-up displays they began to hike along the creek toward a bluff. The planet was stunning with green grasses, trees and blue skies, white clouds and pristine waters. It was hard not to be distracted by such tranquillity.

The patrol climbed to the crest of a hill and lay prone, which seemed odd given they were wearing stealth suits, but it was an instinctive response under the circumstances. The squad leader fumbled at a set of digital viewing glasses and scanned the area but saw nothing to concern them. They spotted an animal of some kind grazing with a calf. It was a light brown colour, with dappled white markings and a shiny black nose. Small velvet like horns broke through the fur behind its ears and it looked up in alarm at some distant sound or smell. Had it seen them? No, it settled back to the business at hand and tore off another mouthful of green pick. The squad leader felt himself salivating at the thought of taking the animal down and butchering it for a genuine meat feast, something he hadn't enjoyed in an eternity, but shook off the urge, signalling his marines to stand and move down the other side of the hill. The quest for resources would now be their main goal.

They descended into a wooded area, walking in a scattered formation as if in a combat zone. It was difficult for all of them not to be overcome by the beauty of this place though. It was indeed perfect in every way. The trees grew tall here and were brimming with bird life; colourful creatures that chirped, screeched and called constantly. Rounding a small hill, they startled another of the grass feeding creature which was alerted to their presence by the sound of their movement. It looked towards them seeing nothing, but its instincts told it to run and in seconds it was gone, so swift on hooved feet. Its meat would probably be a protein rich addition to the Andromedan diet. Everything they saw was recorded on their helmet cams, they need not worry about taking sample material as the data alone could be analysed later via the data being recorded. Their quantum computer programs could discern almost anything from a close range recorded image, hence the need for a ground mission. All they had to do was look around and gather as much data as possible.

They saw a creek, perhaps the same one as where they landed, hard to tell, it certainly looked every bit the same which came as no surprise and the telemetry indicated they should follow it downstream. Its waters rippled and gurgled along at a rapid rate, cascading over flat stones and through reeds. Algae grew at the creek edges and they saw aquatic life, large slow-moving shoals of fish, oblivious to their presence. The creek soon spilled over a small waterfall into the rocky gorge which was easy to negotiate. When they came out the other side a huge valley opened before them. As far as they could see there were green pastures, outcrops of forested areas and a huge river. Across the plains were herds of animals of various sizes, long legged hooved creatures with long slender necks, shorter beasts with striped bodies and near them a pack of doglike creatures.

Their suits were keeping them insulated from the outside, but they could feel that the climate was cooler than home according to their sensors. They pressed on observing as much as they could, focusing on creatures, plants, trees, waterways, rocky outcrops, anything that could provide the resources they required. Analysis of this planet's Moon had already indicated they could harvest some materials there but not everything they needed, so these planetary outcrops may prove vital for the more precious metals they needed to repair the electronics and other components of the ship and its shuttles and interceptor fleet. They took note of the variations in the colouring of the rocks which suggested metallic content. The original computer analysis was proving fruitful it seemed.

Walking through knee high grass, they disturbed a proliferation of insect life, hopping and jumping creatures, winged gnats and flies of various sizes. Scanning the plains, the squad leader noted another creature with a trunk like appendage above its mouth. It was tearing up tufts of grass and shovelling them into its mouth. It was certainly an oddity which all of them stared at for a long time until their attention was broken by another sound, an unnatural sound, mechanical. A plume of dust rose in the air some distance away and the leader motioned for the group to raise weapons and stand ready. They did so without hesitation. A wheeled transport bounced along and then slowed before stopping a very short distance from the marines. When the dust cleared, they saw two beings alight the vehicle, hunters perhaps. Like the Andromedans, these people were bipeds, standing on two long slender legs. They had thin bodies, long arms and five fingers on each of their hands. Their heads were roundish with two eyes above a small proboscis and below that a mouth. What immediately struck the marines was how much they resembled the Andromedans, almost too much of a coincidence. They certainly looked nothing like The Borche. These two wore basic coverings from shoulder to the mid leg joint in a flat green like colour and heavy black boots. One of them was now speaking to the other and two rows of white teeth could be seen flashing under their lips during this exchange. They were close enough to be heard but it was unintelligible to the marines. It was a jabbering conglomeration of sounds cascading up and down with various inflections. It was certainly a complex vocal range. The Titania's computers may well be able to analyse the conversation and perhaps translate the words if they could gather enough data to create a verbal baseline. Figuring out only a few words might be all they needed.

The pair both appeared to be male, one holding something to his eyes as he scanned the area. What were they looking for? As the question resonated in the squad leader's mind it became all too clear, they were counting the animals and recording information about each species. To what end the marines did not understand but they weren't there to solve these questions, just gather intel. Then one of the males pointed towards the marines. He couldn't have seen them, but it seemed like he had. The pair quickly retreated and jumped inside their vehicle, watching the area where the marines stood firm. A sound behind the group caused them to spin their heads. They saw what the two males had taken haven from: a large feline creature, then another and finally a group of five. They were clearly stalking something. The marines held their ground as the creatures came closer. The suits should shield them from these animals visually and screen their scents but if one of these creatures struck a marine, the game would be up. If they moved, the sound would undoubtedly alert the creatures to some kind of presence, and the marines knew not how they might react.

They stood like statues as the first creature slid past the squad. It was a fur covered animal, with huge jaws, the front facing eyes of a predator and a shiny black nose. Its body was slender, light brown and very muscular and trailing behind was a long slender tail which remained low to the ground so as not to alert any prey. It kept low, below the height of the grass. The second and third then the last two of these creatures quietly moved amongst the marines who remained motionless. As the last animal passed a marine its tail flicked the stealth suit. The creature stopped upon feeling the impact and looked back, sniffing the air but then moved on having detected nothing. The group split into two, three going one way and two going the other. The marines watched as the trio worked around a group of hooved stocky creatures around one hundred strong. The other two were out of sight but the marines recognised the tactic. The trio would startle the group into running away while the other two waited and pounced on an unsuspecting victim. Certainly, a highly evolved predatory tactic.

The marines and the two humanoids watched the animals set themselves up. The herd began to move then run and then panic as the predators sprinted after them, then the two that had peeled off in the other direction pounced. In the end they achieved easy kills, taking down two of the unsuspecting bovines. All five predators latched onto the necks of these unsuspecting animals and smothered them to death. Then they began to feast. One then called with a loud roaring sound and several more felines appeared, many young and some larger maned varieties, clearly male given the large testicles dangling between their hind legs. The marines and the humanoids watched as all shared in the spoils, covering their faces in rich red blood as they ate.

The marines and the humanoids waited patiently until the felines were so entrenched that both groups were able to make a stealthy escape. The humanoids started their vehicle, which made barely a sound and slowly edged away from the scene, leaving the animals in peace. The marines stepped slowly away from the feasting creatures, satisfied that their sortie had enabled their cameras and sensors to gather enough information on this occasion. Getting up close to the terrain and life of the planet would give them much more data than a scan from space ever could. They retraced their steps up through the gorges and back along the creek towards the Interceptor. Rounding a hill, they were suddenly stopped in their tracks by a new and substantially more serious threat, one that they were all too aware of. It was a group of The Borche.

The squad leader had to think fast. Borche technology appeared to render the Andromedan stealth capability useless. Given their capacity to overwhelm defences and come through unscathed meant there was little opportunity to analyse these thuggish creatures. The only thing anyone knew was that their technology was highly advanced and they won their battles with little self-regard. If one fell in a fight or was somehow cornered, they would just self-destruct, leaving nothing to analyse or retrieve. Their willingness to die at an instant when in danger led many to surmise that they had a hive mentality and were perhaps driven by an individual leader rather than through a chain of command but again, that was pure speculation.

The squad leader noticed that these individuals, eight of them in this case, were not wearing combat equipment and appeared to be only lightly armed but the fact that they were here was of deep concern and would have to be reported to the Admiral. Right now, though, there was another problem, they were between the marines and the Interceptor, and they would know of the marines' existence at any moment. The marine squad leader unsheathed his side arm as did the others. Whispering via the suit's short-range communicator he ordered them to switch the guns to kill and they raised them, rapid firing at the group of Borche. There was no time for a reaction, not even a chance to be surprised, all eight were down and dead in a few millies. The marines dived for cover fully expecting the Borche to self-immolate but after a few more millies nothing happened. The squad leader looked up, seeing that they lay motionless, dead and bleeding a teal-coloured semitransparent blood. The marines rose from the ground and quickly scanned for more Borche. They tended to counterattack repeatedly if driven back and these marines were all too aware of the tactic but again, nothing happened. It appeared these individuals were alone and thankfully now, very dead.

The squad leader walked towards the bodies and took a long hard look at their faces and contorted bodies. They were much more like animals compared to the hominid like stature of the Andromedans, a truly disturbing race. The nearest thing they could compare them to was a large apelike creature from their home planet but rather than fur or hair, these were scaled and apparently cold blooded both physically and mentally. They did not negotiate nor did they ever retreat. Victory or death was apparently all they knew.

The squad leader then looked into the dead eyes of one of these creatures noticing how they appeared large and round with a green slit-like iris surrounded by a black sclera. The arms were excessively muscular, even on the females and they had no neck to speak of, just a huge, gnarly cranium on a set of very broad shoulders. Their bodies were solid muscle tapering down to the hips which were half the radius of the shoulders and from there rather heavy squat legs. They had a low centre of gravity and ran with a loping gallop rather than a sprint. They were not fast creatures, but they didn't need to be. The squad leader tore his gaze away from The Borche, he didn't have time to speculate. They had to get one of these creatures back to the Titania, just as soon as they scanned it for anything incendiary on the bodies. The remaining seven would have to be hidden. He then considered that they must have a shuttle or some other kind of ship nearby and sent two marines to reconnoitre the area. They had to be sure that they would be able to launch without being detected by any other Borche in the area.

The whole affair was taking much too long but eventually the bodies of seven Borche were covered by creek rocks and foliage. It wasn't perfect but it would do. The squad leader sent two more marines to advise Arda of their discovery and to arrange for the body to be loaded on the Interceptor and taken to Titania. When the first two scouts returned, they advised that there was a ship, a small Borche transport a short distance away. It wasn't being guarded and appeared to be in perfect condition which meant these Borche had not crashed, they had landed here on purpose. Perhaps a pilot and an engineer could be sent back to salvage the machine. Anything they could learn about Borche technology would be highly valuable, but the big question was how the Borche got here and why? That would have to be a conundrum for the Admiral and his officers. The Titania was hardly in any condition to fight, and the squad leader felt a ripple in his gut that he'd felt many times before. No-one wins against the Borche.

It took some time but the marines and their Borche body were somehow loaded onto the interceptor and the craft lifted off unsteadily before heading north. They slipped quickly into the darkness of space and in a short time were cruising towards the moon. As they made their approach Arda was alerted to a warning light on the control panel. She unmuted the radio and heard a garbled array of sounds. Her ship was equipped with a logging device so the sounds were already being recorded. She didn't understand the message, but she knew immediately it was a signal coming from the planet. This mission had indeed turned out to be most interesting.

Learning of the presence of the Borche sent a shockwave through the crew of Titania. They'd travelled here to escape these creatures and now it appeared they'd achieved nothing. Karlou Vardourn was nonplussed, *how* he wondered but there was simply no answer to that riddle right now.

At the debriefing the marines passed on the hard data from their helmet cams, audio from the radio signal and the Borche body. The Admiral, while still shocked that The Borche were on the planet was most pleased with the success of the mission. A salvage crew was despatched to bring back the Borche ship and soon, that too was on Titania. The pilots knew enough about Borche technology to fly the craft. Their space flight systems were almost the same as the Andromedans regardless of any other technological superiority. Perhaps now they would finally gain some knowledge that would enable them to win a fight, should it come to that. Still Admiral Vardourn couldn't stop wondering how The Borche came to be here at all. He shook his head in dismay.

With the scientists and technicians now focussed on The Borche technology, the Admiral turned his attention to the signal recorded by the Interceptor. He watched as the data was uploaded to a translation computer, hoping that it could give them something from nothing. It took almost ten cycles for the computer to crunch the data but eventually the programs were able to offer a rendering of the transmission into some kind of understandable speech pattern. The

Admiral returned to listen as the AI spoke in a metallic monotone voice,

"We are the people of indistinguishable, and we welcome you to our World. We are people of peace and cooperation and would hope to open a indistinguishable with you to learn of your reasons for visiting our planet. The indistinguishable of indistinguishable invite you to make contact by responding to this message on this frequency. We look forward to your response. Peace be with you."

The Admiral looked to his First Officer, Yeovale Darnuth, "What do you make of it?"

"Sounds like an invitation. Nothing threatening at all sir."

"I agree. Draft a response. I think it's time we said hello. Can you translate it into their language?" asked the Admiral directing his question to the technician who achieved the initial translation.

"I believe so sir."

"Very good, see to it."

"Yes sir."

Chapter 7 – The First Meeting

Filo was again at his station listening for any possible reply from the Aliens who they still believed held station behind the moon. Even though his team had only been monitoring for a few rotes he found it to be a most monotonous task and he was starting to get tired of playing computer games and watching documentaries which he couldn't hear well because he had to listen for a live response, even though the recorder was running over everything across the band. As always, he was about to slip into a nap when there was a crackle that fully awakened him in a sec. Filo sat upright just as a dialogue came through that he could easily understand. The aliens were transmitting in the Terranian language! How could that be possible but then he realised they transmitted in Terranian so it would be logical to translate. He then considered how advanced these beings must be to be able to receive, interpret and translate such a message in just a few rotations.

Filo listened, *"Greetings from the people of Andromeda. I am Admiral Karlou Vardourn of the ISS Titania. We have received your message and are pleased that you are open to a discussion about our presence here. I would be very happy to address your leaders and tell you of our travels and that we are no threat to you. We come with peaceful intentions. Alas, it appears there are others who have discovered your planet, and we cannot say the same of them. I would warn you against further transmissions on this band and can offer you an alternative secure transmission system which I can have transported to you. After that we can make arrangements to meet. Please respond briefly to our message so we can decide to send you a transceiver, if indeed our offer meets with your approval. Peace be with you."*

Filo sat for a moment, completely agog. It was a seamless and perfect speech pattern and easily understood. They even had the local accent down word perfect. He then wondered about the "others" that had been referred to and felt a foreboding at the suggestion of ill intent. He snapped out of it and double checked the recorder. The message did not repeat, however he stopped the Terranian transmission after the warning from the Andromedans. He hastily called Jako and relayed the news, and they were soon on a transport with Barkou and Ludic headed back to the League of Governors to report their findings. An emergency session of the Governors was soon arranged and all sat, eager to hear the alien message. Filo played the audio recording without hesitation and the Governors listened. No-one spoke, most holding their collective breaths. There was no mistaking the Andromedan message. They had accepted the Terranian offer.

The League of Governors discussed the message, Garon from the Province of Estonita, Filo's home district spoke first, "We should congratulate Filo, Jako, Ludic and Barkou for their work in this matter. It is truly a great achievement to have contacted beings of another world."

There was nod of agreement and fists hammering the tabletop in appreciation. The representative of the Kaliforn Province rose, "I feel somewhat disturbed by the message.

They say they are here for peaceful purposes and yet they mention a threat. From whom is this threat and what danger does it pose?"

"I agree," added Callon of Afrikaan, "Perhaps we accept the offer of the transceiver to enable communications that will enable them to explain."

The Governors all murmured which opened the door to a debate. It was not heated or hostile as was the way of the Terranian people, but it was clear some were fearful.

"I say we reject their offer and send them on their way," suggested Marron of Pancifica.

"We cannot. Our message was an invitation and what of the threat? Sending them away will not address that issue and we don't know that they will leave. It may just force their hand and we are defenceless." answered Garon.

"That is not entirely true Garon," said Percius of Eropa.

"What does that mean?" asked Garon.

"It means we will do what is best for our people and our planet," explained Percius.

Garon frowned, unsure of what Percius meant but didn't pursue an explanation.

The debate continued and finally a vote was taken. The League of Governors would accept the Andromedan offer and hear what they had to say. Filo would send a reply agreeing to the delivery of the device. A message was recorded and handed to Filo. When he got back to his transmitter array, he loaded the message and pressed transmit…

It was succinct, *"Greetings. The League of Governors accepts your offer."*

As ordered, Filo sent the message once and once only then cut the transmission. The Andromedans asked them to be brief and brief they were.

What now? Wondered Filo

On Titania the Communications Officer received the message and advised the Admiral.

"Very good. Send an encryption device with written instructions; use a probe. Land it in front of the League of Governors assembly building. I believe we have identified the building, have we not?"

"Yes sir," replied the Comms Officer.

"Very good, see to it."

The officer saluted and set to work.

A transceiver was loaded onto a small transport probe with clear instructions. The unit was self-powered, so there would be no complications trying to connect to an alien power source. The Admiral also ordered that the unit and the probe be decontaminated so that there was no chance of infection being spread from the Titania. It seemed the decent thing to do.

This time the Andromedans didn't hide their presence. The probe split the atmosphere with a bright flash and several minutes later a sonic boom shook the halls of the League of Governor sending hundreds of Terranians into the streets and parks to see what had happened. As they scanned the sky a small object glinted in the sunlight and slowly tracked toward the city of Genova. It took station directly above the Government Halls. It then began to move downwards, hissing as its jets pulsed to maintain a steady and purposeful descent. As it neared the ground, three insect-like legs flipped out from the underside of the craft, and it touched down lightly at the base of the vast stairway that led to the main doors of the Halls. The engines ceased and the machine stood for a moment as the Governors watched from the entrance to the Halls of Government. Just then it popped open revealing a device, also black and rather unremarkable. Government workers were despatched to collect the device, picking it up with ease. It was no bigger than a small carry case and very light, a cube shaped apparatus with smooth matt black panels. As they walked back up the steps, the probe closed, fired its main engine and shot skywards, disappearing into the blue in a few short secs.

Many of the people who witnessed the demonstration were quite shocked, but no-one panicked. They had complete trust in their leaders, and it was clear that this…thing…was expected. They also knew that the Governors would share what they knew in due course. No secrets existed on Terrania.

The device was placed on the Governor's conference table. The instructions handed to Garon who noted the precise text, not handwritten but printed on flexible square cards, and smooth to the touch. He read the instructions then looked up at an expectant group of faces, "It simply says we are to switch it on by pressing the small blue button at the top of the device and it will be enabled. An antenna should eject from the unit and seek out the spaceship as the device boots up. It will establish the connection by itself and the channel will open. That's all it says."

"Very well," said Percius, "Press the button Garon."

Garon looked over the black cube noting a single blue button on top and pushed it down. It immediately lit up and, as expected a panel opened and the antenna array rose like a skinny silver serpent and slowly rotated before focusing skyward. The Governors watched as a set of tally lights illuminated on the side of the unit, then two more covers opened whereupon a small black bulbous device popped up from one and a flat disc like item could be seen behind a protective grill in the other recess.

Everyone waited, not really knowing what would happen next. They did not have to wait long as the disc behind the grill began to crackle, "Greetings, this is Admiral Karlou Vardourn of the ISS Titania. I can see that you successfully activated the transceiver, with whom am I speaking?"

In their excitement, the Governors hadn't elected a speaker and for a moment there was complete silence until someone gestured to Garon, "Um, greetings from Terrania. I am Garon of Estonita, one of the Provincial regions of Terrania and a member of the League of Governors."

The other Governors looked pleased with his reply and smiled. Garon felt he'd been very distinguished with his opening reply.

"Greetings Garon, it is good to finally be able to talk. May I firstly apologise if we startled you with our recent arrival. It must have been quite a shock."

"Yes Admiral Karlou, er…" Garon forgot the Admirals full title.

"You may simply call me Karlou or Admiral."

"Yes, of course Admiral. We were certainly surprised by your arrival. We have, until now, known of no other life beyond this planet." Garon spoke with a stiff, deliberate, staccato style of speech given the unusual circumstances.

"That is understandable. We were of the same belief for thousands of generations on our home worlds."

"Where is that may I ask Admiral?"

"It is very far from here, a vast distance from this world, in another galaxy we call Andromeda," explained the Admiral.

"You will have to forgive me, I know little of space and the Universe. I was not the one to detect your presence or to make the initial contact with you."

"I understand. No matter. I'm sure you have many questions. I thought I could address those before we discuss options."

"Options?"

"Yes, but first, let me clear the air, what is it you wish to know about us? The Admiral asked.

The governors looked at each other as Garon indicated with sign language for them all to scribe some questions. He began with the question that everyone wanted answered," Why did you come here?"

"That's a long story," said Admiral Vardourn, "We were forced to flee our home world by an invasive and superior force called The Borche. They swept through our galaxy quickly and efficiently and when we realised, we could not defeat them, we fled, many of us in several directions. Sadly, we fear that billions of our people have been enslaved or killed."

Garon was being handed several questions as everyone listened to the explanation and asked his next question without reference to the notes, "I am sorry to hear that, but we are interested to learn your intentions?"

"That depends. There is much for us to consider but I think the question you need to address right now is how to avoid the same fate we have suffered."

"You are referring to the threat mentioned in your previous communication."

"Yes."

"What is this threat," asked Garon.

"This may come as a shock and I apologise in advance, but we sent a scouting vessel to the surface of your planet, just to see if there were resources that might assist us in the vital repairs needed on our ship."

"What gave you the right?"

The radio system the Admiral sent was a two-way encrypted channel, so there was no fuss with waiting for someone to finish before replying.

"We had no right and for that I once again apologise but while scouting the area we stumbled across a group of The Borche.

We don't know where they came from or why they were here, but they were Borche, of that we have no doubt. Knowing what we do of these creatures, we feel you are in much danger," explained the Admiral with intent, he wanted them to understand the gravity of the discovery.

The members of the League looked at each other wide-eyed and speechless before Garon gathered his thoughts, "What happened to them? Where are they now?"

"They are dead. We had no choice. If they saw us, they would have alerted others and..." the Admiral left the Governors to ponder the probabilities.

"Your people killed them?"

"Yes. It was necessary. You must understand they are not peaceful. They do not respect life except for their own. They take what they want and do so with relentless force. They take no prisoners and will kill without hesitation, including females and offspring."

Someone handed Garon another note which he looked at as he was about to ask his next question but changed his mind and read the question aloud, "Did you bring The Borche here?"

"We don't believe so. The way we travelled and the time it took we feel there was no chance we were followed. No, it appears they were here long before we arrived."

"What do they want?"

"To be frank, we're not sure. This group was unlike any we've come across before. They were not military. We think they were perhaps an advance group of some kind sizing you up."

"So, basically the same as your scouts?" Garon added.

"Yes and no. We were not sizing you up for war, we were looking for a way to repair the damage to our ship."

"Nevertheless, you were scouting our planet for resources just like The Borche."

The Admiral realised this was not a question but a statement and chose his words carefully, "You are right of course. We landed on your planet uninvited and with stealth. I sincerely apologise again. It was wrong but we did not know much about you and did not want to cause a panic by suddenly appearing."

"And yet, that is what happened. We saw you many cycles ago, when you arrived and took refuge behind our Moon. We knew you were here which is why we made contact."

"We assumed so, given your message."

"Never mind," said Garon, "These matters are for discussion later I suppose. I have many questions if you don't mind."

Admiral Vardourn felt some concern that the Governors were dismissing the immediate threat, "And I'm happy to answer them all but I do want to assure you that we are not a danger to you or your planet."

"So, you will leave when the repairs are done?"

"If that is what you wish, then yes." The Admiral lied but it drew Garon back to the issue at hand, "However you do have to face the fact that The Borche know about you and if they come in force, you will be eradicated and from what we can tell, you have no capacity to defend yourselves."

Garon frowned feeling some frustration, "You seem to know more about us than you originally suggested Admiral but how can you be sure we don't have armies and defences at our disposal, hidden from view?"

"We thought of that and we scanned for military signals and hidden bases. You have nothing."

Garon looked to his colleagues knowing the Admiral was right and hoping for some guidance, but all were dumbfounded.

The Admiral picked up on the silence, "We can protect you." Another lie.

"How? You couldn't beat them before and fled. What's different this time?"

"Two things. They do not know we are here and we now, for the first time, have some of their technology. We can use both to our advantage."

"And defeat them?"

"That would be the objective."

"And for this...aid, you will expect certain privileges?"

"That is up to you but if we cannot repair our ship, we cannot fight and I fear we will all be doomed, your people and ours."

"It is not a decision for me alone Admiral. The Governors will have to discuss the matter and with respect we only have your say so about The Borche. How do we know it's not some ruse to illicit cooperation from us?"

"You make a good point so I will send you the coordinates of the site where The Borche bodies are hidden. You have people there, we saw them. They can confirm my story."

"Very well but how are we to understand where you mean?"

"Send us a map with your longitude and latitude data and we will be able to calculate the location from our ship's log. Does that make sense?"

Garon looked around and a few of the Governors nodded, "Yes, we can do that."

"Very well, we will send another probe. I doubt our electrical and computer systems are compatible, but we'll do it the old-fashioned way for now."

Garon knew what the Admiral meant. He required a map on paper.

The conversation went back and forward, each learning more about the other. Questions were asked about the ways of the Andromedan lifestyle, their history and it appeared that there was much similarity between the two histories, regular conflict being the most telling.

"It seems that you have overcome this problem," suggested Admiral Vardourn.

"Yes, we have. It took many rotations to reach a point of consensus. We had to condition all our people to think in a way that made conflict illogical. It was thousands of generations of work and was not easily achieved."

"I envy you. Our people have never known a time when there wasn't war on our home planet or the other planets we ultimately inhabited. So, tell me how you did it? What kind of conditioning?"

Garon again felt uncomfortable with the question and this time the Governors collectively shook their heads. This was not the time, "Perhaps we can discuss that later. It is not a simple thing to explain."

"I understand. Is there anything else you wish to know?"

"Yes," suggested Garon, "What are you?"

This time the Admiral hesitated as he pondered the question, "That too might be difficult to explain. We evolved from inferior species over millions of lifetimes. None of our scientists or anthropologists can really be certain but there was a seminal moment when our species achieved self-awareness, an awakening of some kind and we quickly grew from there."

"I see. We too have developed along similar lines through primates I believe but, alas, many of the historical records were destroyed long ago and we have had to start again in our search for answers. And of course there were those that believed we were created by Gods. I understand that this was very divisive in our history with evolution on one side and creation on another."

The Admiral laughed, "We appear to have much in common, but wouldn't it be interesting if both of our species were in fact created by the same God?"

Garon smiled and started to feel a great liking for this Admiral Vardourn, "Yes, that would indeed be fascinating, but we do not have religion anymore. We have discarded it from our culture. It was the cause of so many conflicts and, without any proof aside from some old texts, we have no reason to consider that this was how we came to be."

"Extraordinary. I am fascinated by your culture. To collectively set aside religion must have been volatile?"

"Not really. As I said, it took a long time to achieve. It didn't happen after a meeting."

The Admiral laughed again, "I like your sense of humour."

"Thank you."

The discussion continued, both the Andromedans and Terranians exchanging questions and answers, some easily dealt with, others not. On the question of physiology, it seemed as though the Andromedan marine's data gathered from the planet's surface was correct when they interpreted a distinct similarity between the two peoples. It was indeed uncanny.

"We should do a DNA comparison," suggested the Admiral.

"Perhaps," replied Garon, "Our scientific capabilities are significant so we should be able to learn much about each other anthropologically. Which makes me wonder, have you overcome disease and other afflictions?"

"Yes, in many cases we have. The basic afflictions most certainly but there are some we cannot overcome yet, such as rampant cellular division caused by all manner of things from toxins to radiation and those handed down through the generations," explained the Admiral.

"We are aware of this too. It was a significant killer in our past, but we have overcome that and all other afflictions. This planet is totally free of disease or affliction in any form."

"I'm impressed. How so?"

"Again, we focussed our resources, on peace and science for the benefit of our people and the planet. We live in total harmony with the environment now. The only way to meet a premature death is misadventure or accident. Longevity here is guaranteed thanks to our scientists."

"Amazing. We would be so interested to learn from you. Perhaps there are things that can be done for our people."

"Perhaps."

Discussions about so many other things were openly exchanged but ultimately there would be a need to get face to face.

"Admiral, the Governors have exhausted their questions for now and will confer to discuss a meeting. Is that agreeable to you?"

"Yes, of course. Just communicate via this transceiver when you are ready. We are constantly monitoring," the Admiral advised.

"We will," then Garon had a thought, "One more thing, how do we know you will not bring with you some form of contaminant? We may well have eradicated disease on our planet, but we have never been exposed to any of your contagions."

"Good question and I am pleased to say we have suits that will protect you from anything we might carry, however I can tell you that we have been isolated in space for a very long time and have not suffered illness for quite some time. That said, some of our people may be carriers so we will carefully screen potential visitors."

"Very good. That is acceptable to us. Thank you, Admiral. We will close now and contact you again soon."

"We will await your communications. Goodbye."

"Goodbye Admiral."

With that Garon pressed the blue button again and the machine shut itself down. He looked to his fellow Governors and smiled but it wasn't a smile that was met with equal joy.

Chapter 8 – The Borche

The Admiral turned from the radio and looked at Yeovale Darnuth, "Well number one, what do you think?"

"They seem amenable. I think we can develop trust. This may be good for us."

"Perhaps, but the presence of The Borche is very disturbing."

"Yes Admiral, it is."

Just then Maneva Gantu, Titania's Head of Medical arrived on the bridge and immediately caught the Admiral's eye,

"Have we learned anything from the body Doctor?" he asked.

"Yes, sir we have. The Borche are quite an odd species. They are or were sequential hermaphrodites."

"Really? Extraordinary in an advanced race."

"Yes. The one we have is male, but it also has dormant female organs which leads me to believe they can change sex when required although I do not know what might trigger such a need."

"Could it be a remnant of their physiological past and they're no longer capable of such change?"

"I don't think so sir, their organs seem too well developed. I believe it is still a primary functionality of the species," suggested the Doctor.

"What else?"

"It may seem odd, but they are physically similar to us. Scans show they have a skeletal structure; all the regular vital organs are not unlike ours but much denser suggesting their home world has higher gravity. Their skin is like animal hide, very tough and almost impossible to cut, even with a medical instrument. My theory is that it's an adaptation to high gravity and heat in their original environment. It protects them. That, or their home world has significant radiation, and their skin protects them from it."

"That makes sense either way. Almost all life forms have adapted to environment and circumstance.?"

"That's true Admiral, and The Borche are certainly examples of such adaptation. Another thing, they have quite large brains, bigger than ours but I cannot tell whether that is because of higher intellect or simply because they are much larger creatures. We know that there are creatures with huge brains that are not very cognitive at all, marine creatures for example but I lean towards them being extremely intelligent given our experiences with them tactically and of course, their advanced weaponry."

"Hmmm. So Maneva, can we kill them?" asked the Admiral

"Despite the lighter gravity of our home world, they are cumbersome due to their bulk. They have no real advantage in lower G; in fact, it may work against them. They must move slowly I think, to avoid stumbling. Another is that they are cold blooded. I can't be sure they're reptilian but the evidence to date suggests it's possible. I'm yet to open the specimen up, so I am only guessing really."

The Admiral pondered for a moment, "Yeovale, do we have access to their attack strategies?"

"Yes Admiral?"

"What do we know about their strategic approach to air and ground assaults?"

"They are selective sir, ground personnel attacking only in the warmer regions while they prefer to attack by air or armoured vehicle in colder climates."

"Which suggests our defence could be as simple as drawing them into a cold climate, limiting their ability," suggested the Admiral.

"Indeed sir."

"Very good," the Admiral said then turned to another of his officers, "Chief of the watch?"

"Admiral!"

"Have we learned anything of their weaponry?"

"Not much sir but I'm hopeful. One thing that does seem to have given them an advantage over us tactically is that their ammunition appears to be self-generating. I just don't know how they do it."

"Fascinating. What of their stealth detection?"

"No clue sir," Narrom Gish admitted, "I cannot find anything on their ship to indicate that any such capability exists. Perhaps it's something they only equip their military craft with."

"Keep working on it."

"Yes sir."

"And Narrom, do it fast"

"Yes Admiral."

The Admiral looked to the floor, deep in thought and then spoke to no-one in particular, "If we can crack their weaponry, maybe produce it for ourselves, we will have the advantage." Then he turned to the doctor once more, "If they are reptilian, can we develop a toxin or something that might eradicate them?"

The doctor hesitated at the thought but then snapped back knowing how The Borche killed indiscriminately regardless of who was in their path, "Yes sir, I believe so."

"Then that is your mission. We need to find a way to not only develop a toxin but a way of delivering it to their ships and their ground forces, something that we're immune to."

"Yes sir."

As the doctor left the Admiral smiled, partly in the hope of perhaps finally having a way to destroy the Borche but also because of his fondness for Maneva Gantu. He snapped out of it instantly, "Ship's status?" he demanded.

"Salvage of all decks is ongoing sir. Repairs continue where materials are available. We have seven active stealth fighters and 10 active shuttles, but I believe we can double that in a few cycles. Unfortunately, we do not have nearly enough marines, most were lost in the rupture of the hull. We will need raw materials from the planet to effect more repairs. The Titania is not battle ready, that will take much longer I'm afraid, sir!"

"Thank you Yeovale. If we can unlock their weaponry and develop a toxin, a way to deliver it undetected we may not need to fight them head on. We need only seek and destroy."

"Those are a lot of ifs, Sir!"

"Very true," The Admiral said as clenched a four fingered fist and lightly hammered his control panel. Despite the odds there may be some hope after all.

The ship's doctor, Maneva Gantu stood over the dead Borche. It had been stripped of its clothing. The first thing she learned was those males and females both had internal sex organs, so on face value it was difficult to tell the difference, but a trained eye could see slight variations. The females were ever so slightly smaller, than the males. Their skin was a little bit duller, and their eyes were somehow softer, if that was even possible. Other than that, they appeared identical in every way. Even though they appeared ape like she didn't believe they were primates.

She walked around the body, which lay flat on its back upon a large metal slab, examining it closely. She looked at the creature's feet, designed to carry a heavy weight and clearly very bony. Five gnarly toes protruded from the fronts of the feet, each with a stubby claw.

The legs were short and heavy, probably adapted for an upright stance. Maneva was no anthropologist, but she considered that their evolutionary development was incomplete as these legs were not adequate for more than short term movement, but she didn't know what the Borche home world was like, so it was perhaps an incorrect assumption.

At the hips she saw a massive protrusion of pelvic bone. It was almost like the legs, and the hips were one part, and the torso, arms and head were dropped in later. It was grotesque. The torso itself tapered up in a widening V which then curved into the armpits. Then the arms, like fleshy battering rams extended almost to the ground. They used these to help lope in a sort of half gallop, like someone on crutches. In attack formation they had to stop to fire weapons, but they had perfected a rolling advance that meant others moved while the shooters were at work and then they swapped. The hands were twice the size of the average Andromedan man with five appendages on each with claws. These were razor sharp and retractable, like a feline. Many a marine glimpsed these slashing personal weapons in their last secs.

The head, like the torso, looked to sit snugly inside a shallow bowl, like an egg in a cup. They looked awkward but the overall fierceness was more apparent. Small holes were all they had for ears; the mouth was wide with rows of tiny sharp teeth and a triangular flat tongue. The nose was a small protrusion of flesh, not much more than a bump with two holes for nostrils and above that those sharp dead eyes. A curved forehead rolled over to a bumpy cranium which protruded like horns.

The beast had no hair at all but was clearly scaled. Maneva tool a surgical knife and teased at a scale, slicing lightly at the indentations that defined its border. They were four-sided scales, sharp at the tip and widening upwards before curving back to a ridge where they grew out, like fingernails. They appeared almost spade like. She teased one off and, as she suspected, underneath was a layer of skin. She pierced the skin and immediately noticed the teal blood ooze from the wound.

"Alright, enough of this play. Let's get down to it. First things first, we remove the brain. Saw please!"

No-one in her medical team spoke as she dismembered the creature piece by piece. The arms and legs were, as suspected, heavily layered in flesh, muscle, sinew and big bones. They were incredibly strong creatures and hard to kill when in their battle dress or in light clothing for that matter. Several direct hits were generally required to effect a kill. Their internal organs were also unsurprising; liver, large heart, two lungs, everything you would expect except that it had an enormous appendix. That prompted Maneva to extract the stomach and look inside. As she thought, mostly vegetable matter. These creatures were not meat eaters unless they had to be. Their teeth were designed to shred foliage, not tissue, but they were very good at both.

The brain was huge compared to anything she'd seen before but not entirely unfamiliar. It has the structure of a ball of lumpy rope, was grey in colour and possessed a frontal lobe, cerebral cortex and other familiar parts. There was one thing though, it had two occipital lobes, one twice the size of the other. It didn't make much sense until she examined the eyes. These were very much unlike an Andromedan eye. They were deeply complex and capable of adjusting to almost any lighting condition but there was more. After dissecting one of the eyes, she could see that the optic nerve was in fact two independent systems feeding into the two occipital lobes. The eye also had multiple lenses which the creature adjusted to the conditions. Whether it did this by reflex, by choice or both she wasn't sure, but she decided this needed more investigation.

By hooking up a small power unit to the nerve she might be able to activate the creature's eye and with another machine, called an optimode she might be able to see what it sees. If she could somehow find the right level of electrical stimulus, then she may be able to trick the eye into working again. What it saw would appear on the screen. She tried a few small level currents to no effect but then on the third attempt the eye flickered to life. On the screen was a blurred image of the wall and operating lights. In a few millies the image cleared as the eye focused quite naturally. She looked at the creature, then put her face in front of the eye. There was an immediate gasp from the team. Maneva kept her head in front of the eye and turned towards the screen, "Oh my word! Call the Admiral immediately."

Admiral Vardourn was quick to respond to the hail, "What is it Maneva?"

"We have found something that might solve one of the puzzles about these creatures, its eyesight."

"What about it?"

"For as long as we have been fighting them, they have always seen through our technology, as if our stealth ships were as visible as a signpost, correct?"

"True."

"And we've assumed that they had some kind of technology that could overcome our own."

"Yes, but we could never crack it and the ship we have in our dock does not appear to possess any such equipment," added Karlou.

"That's because I don't think the technology exists, watch this."

Maneva switched on the optimode, and the eye came to life again. She then stepped into view and pointed to the screen, "There's your answer."

"Oh my," said the Admiral, "Is that…"

"Yes, they have x-ray vision. In fact, I think, given the complexity of their visual cortex and nervous system, they can work across most of the known light spectrum, x-ray, ultraviolet, infra-red, gamma, you name it."

"No wonder we couldn't hide, they could see through our ships, our buildings, everywhere we were."

"And if they combined x-ray with infra-red, it would be impossible to hide under any circumstances. They have the prefect weapon and it's wired into them."

"That also explains why their shielding was totally enclosed, including their faces. They didn't need open helmets because they could see through them."

"Very likely," added the doctor.

"Excellent work Maneva, this will help us greatly. I will inform Narrom so that he may concentrate on their weapons. You must now develop a toxin if you can. Unravel their physiology and find their weakness. They must have one."

"Yes Admiral. That will be my priority however I doubt we'll stumble across it like we did their vision."

"Perhaps not but we might get lucky?" suggested the Admiral.

"They say it happens in threes, so maybe" added Maneva cheekily.

The Admiral smiled and nodded an informal farewell as he left the surgical unit.

Over many sleepless rotes the League of Governor continued to debate the pros and cons of the situation that faced them. On one hand the new arrivals might bring benefits, although everyone struggled to consider what they might be. Others suggested that the technology and warlike demeanour of the Andromedans could send the planet back into a spiral of destruction, something they were sworn to avoid. The simplistic lifestyle they had forged over many millennia had proven beneficial to all on Terrania.

"We must meet with these people, face to face. We need to better understand them before we can make an informed decision," suggested Garon of Estonita.

"That would seem logical," added Callon of Afrikaan, "I would suggest we use their device to convey the invitation."

Most of the Governors appeared to agree when they were interrupted by a minor Government official, "Excuse the intrusion, but we have guests?"

"Guests?" blurted Garon, "The Andromedans?"

"No Garon, they claim to be of The Borche."

There was an immediate dumbfounded astonishment amongst the Governors, and they collectively responded to the news, "Here? Now?"

"Yes, in the foyer!"

"What do they want," someone asked.

"To speak, with you."

There was silence in the hall until Garon said, "Well, show them in."

With that the official scurried through the main doors to bring in the new arrivals.

The Governors murmured, clearly taken back by the revelation, "No sign of extra-terrestrial life for tens of thousands of rotes and now, within a few solar quarters there are two species? Unthinkable," muttered Bayou of Artesia.

They all watched the door in anticipation and within a few mins, the party was shown in. The Governors were taken back by the huge frames of the visitors, which dwarfed even the most robust of the Terranians. Their bodies were covered in suits that shrouded their torsos and faces entirely, only revealing their muscular legs and arms. No-one failed to notice their razor-sharp talons, which were on display. The Terranians were not aware that the talons were retractable.

It was at that moment that Garon remembered the Andromedan communicator, but it was too late to hide it.

The trio of Borche moved towards the Governors and stood side by side clearly looking at each representative with inquisitive eyes.

No-one spoke for the next few mins until Garon decided to break the chill of the moment, "Greetings. I am Garon of Estonita and these are my colleagues. Together we Govern the planet Terrania, welcome."

There was no response initially and Garon was about to continue when a voice bellowed through the Government chambers, "Thank you!"

It was a metallic, raspy voice. It sounded strained and awkward, as if the speaker was struggling to form the words, "We come in peace."

Garon looked around and realised that by speaking up, he had become the designated spokesman for the Governors, again, "Well, that is good news to us all. May I ask of your purpose in visiting us here, today." Garon felt embarrassed by his clumsy words, but it didn't appear to be of any consequence.

"First, we must make something clear to you. We never intended to disrupt your lives here on Terrania. We have no business with you."

"I see."

"However, it has come to our notice that others have arrived that are not of your World and we believe have caused us harm. Are you aware of this?"

The room seemed suddenly colder, and it was clear these Borche didn't mince words or stand on ceremony. Garon felt the question was a demand rather than a friendly request, but it was hard to tell given the awkward translation. He realised he would have to choose his next remark wisely, "Yes, we are aware of another group of visitors. We have not met them as we have yourselves now, but they did communicate through this device," and Garon pointed to the Andromedan communicator.

The trio turned in unison viewing the object, or so Garon thought given they were wearing full faced masks. They seemingly examined the communicator for a moment before turning back to Garon, "We do not care about their equipment, but we do care about our missing comrades. Do you know of this?"

There was another awkward silence and once again Garon found himself forced to answer, "Yes, we have been made aware of this by the others."

The Borche appeared unfazed by the news, "What did they tell you?"

Garon felt uncomfortable about the idea of exposing the Andromedans but a quick glance at the other Governors confirmed that they too wished to avoid any potential conflict with The Borche, "They landed on our planet and while scouting the proximity happened across your, er, colleagues. Apparently the Andromedans chose to attack and kill them all," explained Garon, then he added, "They say they felt compelled to do so because of the history between your two peoples…I'm sorry."

"Your pity is noted but unnecessary. Is there more?" asked the raspy voice.

"Other than the fact that they have a history of conflict with you, no, nothing more."

"And this conflict you refer to, was this a recent event?"

Garon was puzzled by the question, "Um, yes, that appears to be the case, but we assumed you were aware of the war between your people and theirs."

The Borche did not respond to the suggestion, "What are the plans of the Andromedans?"

"They are negotiating for asylum on our planet, having escaped the war."

"And you will grant this?"

"No such decision has been made by the League of Governors. This is not a situation we have had time to absorb or calculate," answered Garon.

"One final question," announced the crackly stagnant voice, "Where are they?"

Garon gulped and wondered if that was noticed by their guests, "Um, their ship is behind our Moon," and anticipating a follow up question he added, "We do not know of their numbers or their military capability. We are a peaceful people with no military. We abhor conflict in any form. We dispensed with wars and the military a very long time ago. We do not wish it to return to our planet."

"But you are conflicted," hissed the apparent leader of the trio, "You were debating the issue of assistance to these people and now we have complicated things for you simply by asking you a few questions, questions you were clearly uncomfortable answering BUT I can also tell you were truthful."

Garon wondered how they could have known what he was thinking and feeling but then added, "We only desire peace and avoidance of conflict."

The trio looked at Garon closely, "We can see that, but conflict may well find you regardless. We will take our leave now," and the Borche began to turn for the door.

Garon watched but then, "If I may, I have questions..."

The other Governors were mortified having been schooled on the ruthlessness of the Borche by the Admiral, but it was too late to shut Garon down. The Borche stopped and look at Garon again, "What is it you wish to know?"

"Thank you. Um, if you will, what are your intentions?"

"That remains to be seen. The killing of our people will need to be answered."

"I see and what of Terrania? Do you seek resources or residence here?"

"We do not require anything from you. This planet does not interest us. You are no threat currently."

"At this time, does that mean..."

"We will leave you alone for the time being, but should you develop the capability to become a threat to us, we will act."

"Is that how it works? You strike against any potential threat even if their intentions are peaceful?"

"Yes. That is how it has been done for millennia."

Garon thought for a moment then asked one more question, "And should we assist the Andromedans, would we then be perceived as a threat?"

This time the Borche hesitated, the trio looking at each other before responding, "That is yet to be determined."

"Perhaps there may be an opportunity to discuss the matter further when you decide?" Garon added.

"Perhaps." And the Borche leader nodded an acknowledgment.

The trio left without further comment leaving the League of Governors in a quandary. The debate about assisting the Andromedans just became much more complex.

There was also the question of advising the planet's populous. One thing that had never changed in all their history was gossip. The Governors, having delivered a bulletin about the Andromedans to the people now needed to make another statement and very soon.

Chapter 8 – Decisions, decisions.

Admiral Karlou Vardourn of the ISS Titania was taking advantage of a brief opportunity to relax in his quarters, reflecting on the events of recent mons. They had lost so much and yet they were on the cusp of success. If they could negotiate a deal with the Terranian people, they would have a new home. The planet would serve them well. It had resources, water, lumber, minerals and a pristine environment. It was uncannily close to the size of their old home world, and the gravity was going to pose no problems it seemed, the first marine patrol was witness to that. Even the atmosphere was good enough to breath without respirators. The good doctor Maneva Gantu had explained, based on her spectrum analysis of the planet, that their respiratory systems would not be at all stressed by the makeup of gases that they would be exposed to. In fact, environmentally, this was a much better world than the one they left, a place that no longer existed in any way they desired...thanks to the Borche.

That thought caused a nervous pang in the Admiral's stomach. How was it that the Borche were here so quickly? Were the Andromedans followed? Surely not, but if so, how? The disaster of their last jump sent their ships into so many unknown areas, some probably flailing light years from here. How could the Broche have known where to go? He pondered the question for some time and somewhere along the way fell asleep in his recliner, a tumbler of beverage falling from his four fingered grasp as his body relaxed. The clink of it hitting the metal floor did not disturb him.

Suddenly, the clanging of a general alarm jolted him awake and a millie later his communicator cracked, "Admiral, you're needed on the Bridge urgently."

He tapped the device on his lapel, "On my way."

Karlou jumped to his feet and felt unsteady as he struggled to overcome the fog of his nap but was soon running to the Bridge only a short distance from his cabin. He burst through the main door and yelled to no-one in particular, "What's the problem?" but before anyone could answer he saw it on the main screen, a Borche ship hovering in perfect firing position, "Someone speak up," he demanded.

First Officer, Yeovale Darnuth responded, "We didn't see them until they were on us sir. They have stealth technology and simply appeared in front of us a few micras ago."

"They didn't just attack?" It was a rhetorical question, but it made the Admiral wonder. This was unlike the Borche. They never hesitated, never negotiated, never took prisoners and never stopped until their enemy was slaughtered, "Have they done anything?"

"No sir, they just appeared and are sitting there."

"Do we have a firing solution?"

"Yes sir. We can shoot if need be?"

"Why didn't we?" the Admiral asked of his number 1.

For a moment Darnuth hesitated then answered, "We cannot win, we are too weak. Besides, they had the advantage and did not take it. That gave me pause."

The Admiral bit down in frustration and thought for a moment, "Hail them."

"Sir?"

"You heard me!" he barked.

"SIR! Yes sir!"

The Admiral's relaxed demeanour of these last few mons was suddenly gone, he was angry and ready for a fight regardless of the odds."

The radio operator clicked at his panel then turned to the Admiral, "You are live sir, all bands."

"This is Admiral Karlou Vardourn of the ISS Titania addressing The Borche cruiser off our forward quarter, please respond?"

There was only the crackle of ether for the next few millies, and the Admiral was about to repeat himself when a metallic voice emanated from the Bridge speaker array, "I am Galek of The Borche, supreme leader in this sector. It is a pleasure to speak with you Admiral."

The statement sent shockwaves through the bridge personnel. This was unprecedented. No Borche had ever communicated or negotiated, in fact no-one had ever heard them speak before and if they had they didn't live long enough to pass on the information. They were killers and everyone on the Titania knew it first-hand.

The Admiral wasted no time responding, "Forgive me for being forward, but I have never spoken to any Borche before. We are not accustomed to pleasantries with your kind. I am wondering why you simply did not attack. That is your nature is it not?"

Those on the bridge squirmed when they absorbed the Admiral's jibe, but no-one said a word.

"Admiral Vardourn, I am not accustomed to being spoken to in such a fashion and I do not believe you have the upper hand here. It was you who killed my scientists was it not? I am here to request an explanation. They were innocent and did not threaten you, true?"

The speakers crackled again as the Admiral formulated a response. He could have lied or pretended not to know but his gut told him that would be unwise, "Yes, we killed them. Where we came from, we were at war with the Borche and they did not give any quarter. We learned the hard way and so, we kill Borche on sight. It has been, until now, the only way we have been able to survive, and I don't apologise for that."

"That is regrettable. I do not know of the troubles you have faced. The Borche have been spreading across the vastness of space for thousands of generations. We have reached a point in our history where there are so many colonies in so many systems that we have lost contact and there are probably many more we simply do not know even exist. Our migratory tendencies are continuous, so colonies create colonies and so on. It would be impossible to maintain contact over the fullness of time and the vastness of space. That is our nature. We are migrants and I hope you can appreciate, we are not ALL merciless. I hope you will take that into account sir!"

The crew gasped. This was not what anyone expected to hear from the Borche. Even the Admiral couldn't help but be rendered silent by the statement.

"Of course, Admiral, if hostilities are required here, I am more than capable of accommodating you, if that is your preference," added Galek.

All eyes were on the Admiral; he turned to his First Officer who simply shrugged. His next remark may determine the fate of what could very well be the last of his race living in freedom. The Borche will have, by now, conquered all the Andromedan territories and planets and the survivors would live out the lives in servitude. Trust would be hard to develop with these beings. He pressed the communicator button and simply said, "I'm listening..."

"We desire a parley with you, face to face to discuss your arrival in this sector and your intentions. We are at peace here and do not desire nor search for conflict BUT rest assured we will deal with any threat we face. It is my hope that you do not pose such a threat however there are those amongst us who are already of the opinion that you should be eradicated after the killings on Terrania. I want to give you the opportunity to explain yourself before we decide, how say you?"

"What you are proposing sounds more like a trial. I confessed to the killings and I explained why. I am no more a threat to you than you are to me. I accept your explanation of the Borche migratory habits and the likelihood that your approach to life is much less hostile than the Borche we encountered in our home galaxy. With that as a consideration I am prepared to parley, but not to stand trial."

"Fair statement," said Galek, "I therefore invite you to meet me as a guest on board the vessel Quaal for a frank and open discussion. The Universe is vast Admiral. There is room for us all."

The Admiral gave his First Officer a signal to stand down and clicked the comms again, "I accept. When shall we meet?"

"Right now, is as good a time as any. We are here; you are here and not going anywhere from my observations. Please Karlou, come meet with me and we shall talk."

The Admiral didn't miss the personal touch, *very clever*, he thought, "I'm on my way," he snapped and closed the communication channel.

Yeovale Darnuth said, "It's a trap Admiral, I can feel it. Don't go."

"I must. If I don't, we're dead anyway. Take over here and be ready."

"For what?"

"Anything!"

He called for Maneva Gantu who promptly arrived on the Bridge and explained the situation to her, "You will accompany me. You may be able to learn something more about the Borche physiology and how we can deal with them if we need to."

"Yes Admiral," she said with much trepidation.

"Chief? Muster a task force, fully armed to accompany us. They may be demonstrating tolerance but I'm not buying it. I want us to have a fighting chance. And a fighter escort with the shuttle if you please."

"Yes sir!"

Everyone was thinking that such an approach might be seen as inflammatory to the Borche but who in their right mind would meet them unarmed?

The arrangements were swift and within a cycle the Admiral and the doctor were on route to the Quaal to meet Galek of The Borche. Few words were exchanged as they approached the vessel. It was an imposing ship, dark and foreboding, almost twice the size of the Titania. Karlou scanned the vessel. It reminded him of a great marine animal from his home planet, a huge, bulbous front end where he envisaged the bridge and main control systems to be located. The bulge tapered back to a cylindrical mid-section where it appeared the transport systems were housed and behind that engineering and at the rear the engines. Accommodations were probably set throughout the ship to enable easy access to the various tasks of the crew. It seemed logical. He also noted that this vessel was built for long haul travel and to fight. The engines, while somewhat obscured by their angle of approach were clearly hyperspace capable and Karlou didn't need to be reminded of Borche firepower. The ship was encrusted in defensive weaponry, much of it far superior to anything the Titania had and, for that matter, beyond that of the Borche he had fought. Clearly these Borche were more advanced than those that attacked the Andromeda Galaxy. He knew that a fight here would be futile even if they had a hundred ships of the Titania's calibre.

He turned to Maneva, "We cannot defeat these people in armed conflict. Look around, learn as much as you can without making it obvious. If we need to deliver a package, I want it to be effective. I assume you have been working the problem?"

"Yes sir," Maneva kept her response official given the circumstance and the mixed company on the shuttle, "I am making progress Admiral."

"How soon?"

"One or two dars. Having their DNA has made the task quite a bit easier. They are sentient beings and much like us in so many ways, but the differences are enough to work in our favour."

"Very good." He then turned to his task force, "Keep your weapons down and with repressors on. We will not shoot except in self-defence, understood."

There was a collective "YES SIR!"

The shuttle pilot steered towards a strobe beacon amidships. There was a sudden glint as they approached. The vessel had a smart shield which would have evaporated them had they been designated hostile. The Admiral was relieved but none of them would have known about it had the Borche decided to erase them at that moment.

The stealth fighters on each side of the shuttle were also allowed through which suggested the Borche were expecting an armed escort. The trio of craft slipped through an opening in the hull which was protected from the vacuum of space by another shimmering field of some kind. Again, a technological superiority that the Andromedans had only seen in Science Fiction. Karlou wondered how they were able to do it.

Inside, the vastness of the Quaal became obvious. The landing area was massive. Strobe lights on the deck guided the pilots into a landing zone where they all touched down with loud clanks. They cut their engines and prepared to exit wearing suits just as their ground patrol had done on Terrania to avoid contamination.

The exit door of the shuttle hissed open, and the marine detachment alighted first doing a quick check before Karlou and Maneva stepped onto the flight deck of the Quaal. The Admiral looked around. He saw a huge openness and layer upon layer of decking accessing various levels of the ship. Numerous vessels of all types were housed here, fighters, transporters, carriers, small cruisers. The Quaal was not only a huge battlecruiser, it was a maintenance facility, a self-sustaining fortification. As he looked around, he noticed the Quaal's personnel peering at their tiny shuttle and stealth interceptors which were dwarfed by the cavernous interior of the Borche ship.

Moments later a wheeled transporter sped to the Andromedans where a driver and escort met them, "This way if you please," came a crackly voice via the electronic translator.

No-one spoke but they did respond, taking their seats on the machine. No mention was made of the armed Marines, two of which accompanied the Admiral and the Doctor while the remainder took station with their craft. The seats in the transport were too big, given the bulk of the Borche but they were comfortable enough. Maneva noted the temperature within the ship, it was much hotter than Andromedans were used to and the humidity was almost at saturation point, *interesting.* She double checked her wrist scanner to make sure it was recording the data...it was.

The shuttle sped through the ship at high speed, flashing past an array of workshops, cabins and all manner of facility that you would expect on a fighting vessel. Their arrival had certainly piqued the interest of the Borche crew who lined the transport corridor to catch a glimpse of these strange aliens. After fighting these creatures so recently it was odd to now be a fascination to a group of the same species who were oblivious to their existence until now.

The transport came to an abrupt halt inside a small square room, a door clinked shut behind the shuttle and within an instant they felt the room rising. The elevator was as swift as the shuttle and within a handful of millies the front of the box opened, and the transport shot forward, winding through living quarters, mess halls and what seemed to be entertainment facilities. Many Borche were seen lazing in what appeared to be sunrooms, basking it would seem. As far as the Admiral could see, life on board the Quaal was just like any he had served on back home. Another lift and another speedy zig zag and a sudden halt saw them arrive at a pair of doors which immediately slid open. Within they saw a party of Borche, heavily armed and in full dress uniforms which the Admiral recognised except these were far more advanced than anything he ever faced during the war. The Admiral and his entourage were ushered politely through the door and into the room, which clearly had one purpose, to meet and talk.

"Welcome Admiral," came a familiar metallic crackle, "I am Galek." The Borche leader emerged from behind his guardians festooned in a robe of many colours which the Admiral considered must have been ceremonial. It didn't ease his tensions.

"Thank you, Galek," replied the Admiral. He looked over the Borche leader. It was unusual to see one of them without battledress and to see the face of such an individual. They were always covered in combat.

"Please Admiral, join us for a parlay. I'm sorry we have nothing to offer by way of refreshment. We were uncertain of your requirements, but I see you are taking all precautions anyway. We don't know what pathogens we might exchange on our first meeting. Very wise indeed."

"Thank you," replied Karlou. He wasn't about to engage in too many pleasantries until he knew where this conversation was headed. He settled into a large chair, ornate, wooden he suspected but not a tree species he was familiar with.

Galek looked at Karlou through his large black slitted eyes, "I see there will be no small talk so we will get down to business if you prefer."

"Yes, please."

"Very good," Galek clapped his clawed hands once and his guardians disbursed to designated positions around the perimeter of the room. The admiral noted that the design enabled for each to be in a perfect firing position and no matter where his marines turned, they would always have a gun behind them, "So Admiral, should we start with a discussion about your arrival in my sector. What brings you here?"

Karlou adjusted his position in the seat while he considered an answer, "I hope you won't be offended but we have just escaped a savage war with your people and are not feeling overly...trusting of your kind. My people have lost much, so trust isn't easily given. Answering that question at this juncture would be premature."

"I understand Admiral but, as I explained, the Borche you fought are unknown to us and are probably a faction of a faction. We have explored and settled many areas and at times, come across our own kind and had to fight for survival ourselves. We are not all the same, that's what I am trying to say," explained Galek.

"I understand that Galek, I'm sorry I do not know your title? Would you prefer I use 'supreme leader'?"

"Galek is acceptable. I've never been comfortable with titles."

"In that case you should call me Karlou."

"Very well Karlou, please continue."

Despite the metallic translation and the odd accent, the Admiral gleaned that Galek was an amiable character. Still, they were Borche and getting past the bitterness of war would not be as simple as a few pleasantries, "May I ask then Galek, how did you come to occupy this region?"

"We have been here for generations. The way we came here was peaceful. We found no hostiles when we first came. We did come across several occupied Worlds and some we took for ourselves. Others we left to their own devices, but we occasionally check in on them," Galek explained.

"Check in on their technical progress; like a threat assessment?"

"Yes, that would be accurate."

"Is that why you are here, visiting Terrania?"

"Indeed."

"And what was your assessment?"

"That is ongoing and our scientists, the one's your people killed, were part of that process but the Terranians remain inert. They pose no threat to us."

"So, you will simply leave them alone?"

"Yes, their planet is of no interest to us. It is excess to our needs in this region, and it is too…cold, even in the equatorial regions. We would not find it at all hospitable. And we simply do not need another world for our people."

"I see. In that case, our arrival must now provide a potential threat. We are much more advanced than the Terranians militarily and we are capable."

"True, but you would not win. Our numbers are many and our technology superior. You could not at all defeat us. I grant you there would be some blood shed on our side, but it would be superficial, true?" Galek didn't wait for a reply and continued, "And I suspect Karlou that you are not the kind of leader who would launch a full-scale attack knowing it would result in total annihilation. I think your intentions are otherwise focused, hmmm?"

"As I have stated Galek, we are here because of your people. We barely escaped with our lives and left many more to die or become enslaved by the Borche. So, yes, my intentions are to find somewhere new to call home and I thought we found it here. Am I now to be told otherwise?"

"That remains to be seen. It will not be up to me entirely. It will require a gathering of our clan masters, and a vote. Of course you will be offered the opportunity to state your case."

"I see; we have come into your territory and so, to stay we must put up a case and be heard by The Borche who will decide our fate?"

"Sadly Karlou, that is the case. Your arrival is somewhat unprecedented in our local history. Most liveable planets here have only plant and or animal life. Those that are occupied are under Borche rule and this one," Galek gestured toward a window towards Terrania, "is occupied by an indigenous species that, after thousands of periods of internal conflict, has chosen peace and prosperity for itself. Had they left their planet and turned those aggressions onto us, the world down there would be very different indeed."

"I see and what happens if your clan leaders decide we are too big a risk?"

"Karlou, you have a preconceived idea of our people and not without good reason. Your planet…"

"Planets!"

"Apologies, your planets were unfortunately the targets of a rogue element of Borche. That would be my basic assessment. We are not alike. Please understand that. Yes, we have become what we are through aggression and occupation, but it has been strictly a self-defence approach and not one of conquest."

"I would argue that taking a pre-emptive approach is not self-defence; that has not been my experience, and I certainly didn't expect to arrive here having to suddenly speak for the future of my people," Karlou added.

"I understand that but that's exactly what you will have to do. You are in our territory. You have acted with hostility toward the Borche, albeit based on bitter experience but if you think about it, you have come here and done exactly what the Borche did to you."

The Admiral considered the remark, "That's a stretch Galek, we killed a mere handful of your people, that is not genocide."

Galek paused, "I concede your point Karlou."

The Admiral decided to get to the point, "OK, what are our options. Whether I like it or not, we are here and we cannot simply leave. Our resources are virtually spent. All we seek is a home, somewhere our people can prosper. We are done with war against the Borche and ourselves."

"That is exactly the kind of thing you should say to the clan. They are not unreasonable Karlou. If you agree to this, the killings on Terrania will be forgotten, I assure you."

"How can you guarantee that? I know what my people would do under the same circumstances. The value of life is paramount, and we would not sweep it aside," Karlou suggested.

"Perhaps Karlou, the value your people put on one life is far more significant than the value we put on ours. You see murder while we see casualties. It is not the same to us."

The Admiral was a little surprised. How could a species become so prosperous and advanced without putting life at the fore?

"What say you Admiral," Galek reverted to Karlou's official title suddenly, "Will you give us a chance to give you hope?"

Karlou looked at Maneva, but she shrugged, clearly as confused as he was. He looked at the floor and nodded his head, "Alright, I will."

"Excellent. We will make the necessary arrangements and contact you when the time comes.

The meeting was short, but no-one was left wondering where they stood. As the Admiral followed Maneva into the shuttle he asked, "Did you learn anything?"

"Yes sir."

"Good."

Chapter 9 – Strategies

In her lab Maneva Gantu examined some slides under her microscope when the Admiral showed himself in, "Am I disturbing you?" he asked.

"Not at all."

"Good. I want to run something by you."

"Of course, Karlou," There was no need for formality here, "What is it?"

"Our meeting with Galek, was there anything odd about it?"

"Aside from the fact that they seemed to be somewhat civilised, no not really but I can tell that you feel otherwise," suggested the Doctor.

"Well, yes. They didn't ask about the bodies of their scientists."

"Perhaps they have already been retrieved?"

"Perhaps, but that would have raised questions about one of them not being amongst the dead."

"A valid point but Galek said they do not put the same value on life as we do. It's possible that the deaths are just a hiccup and they don't care about the bodies. You confessed to the killings and that might be enough for them…maybe."

"That's a big maybe. If they suspect we have a body, that could count against us, but we cannot now simply say here's a dead scientist. Sorry about the state of it, we were looking for ways to kill you."

Maneva laughed, "I'm sorry Karlou. Your ability to make light of any situation has always amused me."

"Believe me, I didn't mean to be funny, but I do think they have a different attitude. Even when we fought them, they didn't respond to a wounded comrade, they left them to self-immolate. They never needed to retrieve bodies because there weren't any. They just pressed on relentlessly until they won or were all dead."

"In which case what Galek said makes sense, they don't value life like we do. If they have the same approach to life outside of conflict, then it could be helpful. They may not be as careful as us and therefore less likely to anticipate a deception," Maneva suggested referring to Karlou's request for a way to kill the Borche, "But if they are suing for peace and could offer us sanctuary, why would we go ahead with an attack on them?"

"Because I simply don't trust them. Call it instinct or just experience. I've seen what they're like in combat and I cannot simply accept that these Borche are not made of the same stuff," said Karlou.

"I see," Maneva wasn't convinced.

"Look at it this way, should we drop the only advantage we might have on the say so of one Borche individual? He might be the exception to the rule and then what? I want to keep all my options open."

"I understand," conceded Maneva.

"So, tell me what you have learned. Have you got a strategy in mind?"

"More than that Karlou, I have a solution I think."

The Admiral's eye went wide with surprise and anticipation, "Do tell."

"Well, I took readings from their ship. Their environment was very hot and humid. I saw humidifiers in many parts of the ship. I believe they originate from a sultry world, which might explain their hardened exteriors. They have adapted to an environment that is somewhat hostile. I would describe their outer hide as a protective coating," she explained.

"What are they protecting themselves against?"

"Fungus!"

"What?"

"I think they are susceptible to fungal infections. When I removed some scales and exposed the dermis of the dead Borche to our atmosphere it quickly became a haven for a variety of infections. In fact, by touching the dermis with my bare finger, I infected that piece of skin with staphylococcus. We carry these infections on us all the time, but they only attack us if we are in a weakened state or have an open wound, but the Borche seem to have no resistance at all," Maneva explained

"Fascinating, but if their hides are built to withstand any such invasive affliction, how do we deliver it?"

"That could be as simple as an aerosol. Their environment is perfect for delivering a pathogen which they could inhale. I think attacking them from the inside is the key. They would simply be overcome by the spores."

"And how fast would it be? We must incapacitate them quickly, if need be."

"If I'm right, it would be rapid. They would never have been exposed to irritants like those that we carry. I believe a volatile cocktail of these pathogens strategically released throughout their ship would be swift and effective."

"So, we would have to go back and deliver it rather than fire a projectile?"

"I imagine Admiral, that firing anything at such a ship would meet with a lethal response, so yes, a repeat visit would be the only way."

"Well, they didn't seem phased that we took armed Marines on board their vessel which says to me they are very confident that we pose no threat or are simply too weak to be a concern. That too gives us an advantage. How would we deliver the strike?"

"Many ways, aerosol or even a gel which would simply disburse quickly into their environment, preferably near ventilation intakes. It's not that difficult, like leaving a window open," Maneva suggested.

"Would they not have scrubbers?"

"Perhaps, but I don't think they would expect to be exposed to anything like this in space. They may simply use dust filters and nothing more. Our pathogens are microscopic, so they would mostly pass through a dust filter I think."

"How long do you need? And how many for a ship as big as the Quaal?"

"Hard to say. Growing the fungus isn't difficult. If we could find their central air conditioning systems, that would probably be enough. We would only need to infect a small number initially and it would spread quickly after that I believe."

Karlou nodded, "Get back to work, I want as many gel, um, what do we call these things?"

"Gelvaps, they evaporate and release the spores."

"I want as many Gelvaps as you can produce in four dars. I doubt we have much more time than that."

Maneva frowned, "It sounds like you are planning a pre-emptive strike, are you?"

"No, I just want to be ready, for anything. Hopefully nothing but..."

"I understand; we'll work until they're ready Karlou. You will have enough."

"Thank you Maneva," and he smiled and bid her farewell. How could he tell her that a pre-emptive strike was probably the only option available to them if they were to survive?

The League of Governors were still struggling with the reality of their situation. For all their known time they thought they were the only sentient beings in the Universe but now there were three intelligent lifeforms and all were either on or in the vicinity of Terrania. What to do?

"The Borche are no threat to us if we maintain neutrality. If we ever go down the road of building arms again, they have made it clear that it will be dealt with," said Marron of Pancifica.

"Those are good points," replied Percius of Eropa, "but I am incensed by the Borche holding dominion over us like it is their right. This is our planet and our way of life. What gives them the right to dictate terms to us?"

Most of the Governors thumped the tabletop in agreement of the statement.

Bayou of Artesia further added, "One thing that the Borche may have solved for us is how to deal with the Andromedans. How can we make an agreement with the enemy of the Borche? We cannot! I feel the debate is mute now. The Borche and the Andromedans should be left to sort out their own disagreement in whatever way they see fit, and we should go on without any further need to be a part of it."

Again, a thumping of fists gave his remarks endorsement.

"So, are we to sit back and do nothing? We have already communicated with the Andromedans, and they wish to meet with us. They are more like us than the Borche. I do not feel that casting them off is of any benefit," said Garon, "Further I believe we need to keep the Andromedans onside. If the day comes when we must fight off the Borche, having them here would be a benefit."

The mixed reaction indicated to Garon that his argument was not convincing.

"We have for as long as anyone can remember, been a peaceful planet, a cooperative people and that is how it should stay. I say we reject any suggestion of asylum to the Andromedans and leave them to the Borche," called Vanis of Carthidge.

"That is easier said than done Vanis. The Andromedans have delivered us a communication device and will, no doubt, expect us to contact them again soon. What are we to say? We feel that the risk to our planet with the arrival of the Borche is too high a risk and we want you to move along?" asked Garon.

"Yes, that is precisely what I am saying. We owe them nothing; we did not invite them. They simply arrived," added Vanis.

"You all heard the Borche," Marron of Pancifica said, "they will not accept the people of Terrania weaponising. If we become a threat to them, they will intervene. We cannot afford that. I feel we must maintain neutrality. Leave the Andromedans to the Borche."

"But what if the Borche are a worse prospect than the Andromedans? We send them on their way and the Borche decide to enslave us, what then?" asked Bayou of Artesia.

The debate went around, frustrating all involved until a resolution was drafted, a vote finally taken and by a casting vote it was decided that the Andromedans would be given one last hearing to answer the issue of the Borche and how they plan to proceed.

After the vote it was Garon who pushed the button on the communicator. It took some time for the Admiral to answer, "It's good to hear from you Garon. Have the Governors decided?"

"Yes Admiral, they have. We request an audience with you to discuss the Borche. They have made their presence known to us and, well, not to mince words, presented us with an ultimatum. We feel uncomfortable with it, but we are in no position to argue. What say you?"

"When can we meet?"

"Tomorrow at the half rotation. I hope you understand our system of time?"

"Yes Garon, we have worked it out. You are talking about the middle of the day. I will be there tomorrow," suggested the Admiral.

"Very good, we will see you tomorrow," Garon concluded and the communicator was shut down.

He looked around the room at his fellow Governors. None of them seemed overly pleased but they had to know what the Andromedans were thinking so they could make a fully informed decision.

The following day at the designated time Admiral Vardourn and his First Officer, Yeovale Darnuth along with Maneva Gantu touched down in a shuttle on the parkland next to the Government halls. They were met by staff of the League and escorted to the main chamber. Again, they wore suits to avoid spreading or receiving pathogens.

"Welcome Admiral, I am Garon."

Garon extended and arm in what the Admiral gleaned was some kind of ceremonial gesture and did the same. Garon smiled and grasped the Admiral's hand, noticing that he was only four fingered. He resisted the urge to pull away, "Our customary welcome is to shake hands. No-one can remember why we do this, but it has something to so with our overcoming hostilities in the past."

"I see; it is a good custom Garon. Let me show you ours," and the Admiral stood to attention crossed his chest with his forearm and a closed fist, "It is also a gesture that was also developed through conflict as I understand it. It defines strength and discipline."

"It does certainly demonstrate power Admiral."

"Please Garon, let us not stand on ceremony, call me Karlou."

"Very well and your colleagues?"

"This is my first officer Yeovale and the ships doctor, Maneva."

"A female?" Garon could see her womanly shape under the skintight suit," Impressive. We were under the impression that your military was predominantly male. We stand corrected," Garon said with a slight blush.

"On the contrary, our military has always been a mixture of male and female personnel. They all contribute equally," explained Karlou.

"Even in times of hostility?"

"Yes indeed. The females are every bit as good, if not better fighters than them males of our race. It surprises you?"

"Certainly. Our people have a very different approach. As you know we don't have a military but if we did, it's not at all likely that women would be expected to fight, although I do believe it was very different in the past. We have corrected that anomaly."

Karlou felt astonished at the claim, "How did you make the correction as you call it?"

"Simple, we returned to the ways of our ancestors. Men work and women raise the family. The roles are indoctrinated in our society. You see, our past, like yours was built on conflict and conquest and it almost destroyed us. We chose to rebuild our way of life with a simplistic approach and that included the roles of the sexes," Garon explained.

"Hmm, that might be something the females of our world would struggle with. They are very much accustomed to their independence."

"I'm certain that they are but we don't see it as our men being superior or the women being inferior, we all have our roles to fulfil for the benefit of the race and the planet. It has served us well for millennia."

"I am not disputing your philosophy Garon. I am simply trying to understand how it works. Clearly it does, don't misunderstand, but it would be something our people would have to adjust to."

"Perhaps, but it took generations for us to reach this point. It wasn't something we just decided to do one day and things changed. Sometimes the changes that are necessary are the slowest to prosper, don't you agree?"

"I do," said Karlou.

"Our first frank conversation. Most interesting and enjoyable. We have much to learn from one another I think Karlou. Don't you agree?"

"I do and I hope we can have many more such discussions."

"That's good to know," Garon said as he swept a glance across the other Governors, "but first we need to address the issue at hand, and that is the Borche. As I mentioned yesterday, they have made their presence known to us. In fact, they appeared here, a trio who communicated with us quite directly. I would go as far as saying their attitude was one of an ultimatum," suggested Garon.

"That sounds very much like the Borche. We have met with them too."

"You have?" said Garon who couldn't hide his astonishment.

"Yes, they confronted us and we went aboard their ship," Karlu hesitated then asked, "I feel that our presence was not something they could have known without some assistance. I do not wish to start our dialogue on a negative note, but did you reveal us to the Borche?"

Garon didn't hesitate, "Yes, we did, in fact I did. There was no lying to them as far as we could discern and we must think of our people first and foremost. We did not wish to gain an enemy. I hope you can understand that."

"I do understand and I don't blame you. You were no doubt in an impossible situation. To suddenly be confronted with two opposing life forms and on your own doorstep, that must be something of a shock," Karlou added, while quietly seething at the news. On the other hand, what choice did they have?

"I, we, are so glad you understand. It was not something that sat well with us."

"Nevertheless, we are now forced to negotiate with the Borche, not something that we've ever faced before. Our past with them has been nothing but hostile and there was no negotiation. Their only goal was total obliteration, and the survivors became their slaves. That was not acceptable to us, as I'm sure you can appreciate."

"Of course. I am sorry, but they showed no such aggression to us."

"Nor us, surprisingly but they certainly made it known that we would have to adhere to their will if we were to avoid any conflict and while I want to avoid conflict, I do not feel obliged to wilt to their demands. That isn't our way," Karlou said.

"I understand what you are saying and I feel the same way, but I am speaking from a personal point of view and in the interests of transparency, I have to add that not all within the League are in agreeance with me."

"I see. Then we have much to discuss, don't we?"

"We do; shall we be seated?" Garon suggested and motion to the meeting table.

With that the Governors and the three Andromedans took their seats and the meeting began in earnest.

When all were settled in their respective places and formal introductions completed, the discussions began. Garon had clearly been elected or fallen into the role of chairing the negotiation, if that's what they were, "I feel that this issue of the Borche is one that we must address before anything else can be decided, do you agree?"

Karlou looked around the table and even though he had never met with the Terranians before, he could easily see who was with him and who wasn't. Their facial features and body types were so very close to those of the Andromedans it was uncanny. He wondered if God had somehow managed to create two worlds. Maybe he got it right with these people? "I said before we can protect you and we will if that time comes but I think before we can deal with the Borche, we need to know if it's worth our while. Is Terrania willing to offer us anything for such protection?"

"We have discussed that very intensely and you are here by the thinnest of margins, so it's not as simple as saying yes. Perhaps you can suggest what it is you desire and we can go from there?"

"Certainly," Karlou cleared his throat and shifted in his seat. These kinds of negotiations were for diplomats, not admirals but the diplomas weren't here, "We, the remainder of the people of Andromeda formally seek asylum on Terrania. Our home is lost; we identified your planet as a potential home. We did not know if there was life here, let alone highly evolved and intelligent life but here you are. We are not sorry about that, we are glad. I think, given our similarities, there may be opportunity for our species to prosper together, learn from one another and live together in peace and prosperity. I ask that you put the issue of the Borche aside for a moment and consider our position and look at this as an opportunity to join two great societies."

Garon was prepared for the pitch and didn't refer to the others for advice, "That may be so Karlou, but your history is one of significant hostility is it not? How do we know you won't fracture what is essentially a pristine existence in a perfectly balanced environment?"

"You make a very good point, but I can guarantee that we do not desire conflict, we never have. We are merely soldiers doing our duty. If there is no conflict, then we are not going to look for it. We desire peace above all. To be frank, all the recent conflicts I have endured through my career have been defensive actions. The people of my planet have had their troubles, but I can categorically tell you that the people I represent have NEVER been the antagonists."

"Very well, we'll take you at your word Admiral. Thank you. Of course we cannot simply say yes. This is a request without precedence and one that will indeed have an impact on our planet and our people. We would need to find you suitable dwellings, you would need to meet our standards and our laws, as basic as they are. You would ultimately have to forego your weapons for example. Our society has, through thousands of cycles of conflict come to realise the futility of it and taken a long time to reseat the minds of the people to achieve enduring peace. This is something we value more than anything and, whether you agree or not, you are a risk to that," Garon sternly suggested.

"Garon, we understand that and we are in full agreement. We do not desire to continue our old ways. We desire what you have but not at the cost of prosperity."

"And yet you offer to be our defenders. Is that not a continuation of your old ways?"

The Admiral was not yet willing to share the details of his conversation with the Borche, but it was clear that their options were becoming limited, disarmament either way but he preferred to do so on Terrania over some designated Borche planet, if such a place even existed. He doubted it did. He would have to tread carefully, "Yes Garon, I offered to be a protector but there may be another option. You have met the Borche and they have made their position clear. We too have met with them and both of us agree on one thing, we don't like ultimatums yet that is what they lauded over us. There's an old saying in our history, the enemy of my enemy is my ally. We must be allies now that the Borche have declared an interest in this system, your planet. If we can agree on that we can then decide how best to deal with the Borche. Do you agree?"

"The Borche say they have an interest in our planet?" Garon asked.

"Only in that they deem Terrania as part of their territory," Karlou suggested and he wasn't lying this time. He had very cleverly created a point a deference which he hoped would win some sympathy and support from the doubters and from the reaction, it worked. The Governors all murmured and whispered amongst one another which caused Garon to pause. Karlou wondered if he would stick to the script now.

"You make an interesting point Admiral, and it is one we have discussed and to be frank, are still very much divided on. Some here want to reject you completely and send you on your way. Others feel we need allies against any such threat from the Borche while another party feels this might antagonise them. They themselves have not indicated clearly how that might be received but it was inferred that assisting you could put our planet at risk," Garon explained.

Karlou saw an opportunity, "I would table this as an option then. We appear before the Borche and tender them an offer; that we disarm and find residence on Terrania. We further offer to hand over all our weapons and our ship to the Borche, guaranteeing to them and to you that we seek no conflict now or in the future. We make them this offers on the basis that they guarantee amnesty to Terrania for all time. If you agree to such a deal and they in turn, accept it, the rest is incidental."

It was a gamble, but he had to think fast. He looked at Yeovale, but he couldn't tell what reaction was hidden behind his helmet. He looked at Maneva and could tell she was smiling. He then looked at the faces of the Governors. Many a frown had disappeared. He felt good, the offer was sound.

Garon opened the offer to the Governors for some frank discussion. It wasn't going to be a simple task taking in ten thousand of newcomers. What impact might such a jump in numbers have? After much more discussion and calm debate with a few more guarantees thrown in a vote was taken and, despite some tokenistic reluctance, the majority agreed to the proposal, with contingencies.

Garon then turned to Karlou and smiled, "If you can make such a deal with the Borche then you have a deal with us. The rest, as you say, can be negotiated later."

The Admiral shook hands again the Garon and felt a great deal of relief. He now had something to work with and, having seen the Quaal also felt he had one more significant bargaining chip that could turn the whole deal in his favour.

Chapter 10 – Plans within plans

Admiral Vardourn relaxed in his cabin pondering the meeting with the League of Governors. His fast thinking turned out to be an exceptional piece of statesmanship for a military man, with many agreements reached. Now all he had to do was meet with the Borche and play the game again. He had no idea how they might react to his idea, but he didn't really care, if things didn't go well, there were other options being developed. Even if the Borche agreed to his deal, he didn't really trust that they would honour it long term. He had no evidence of course, except for his military experience with their kind back home, but that was more than enough, and he simply didn't believe that these Borche could be far different in real terms and they were clearly willing to kill if anyone overstepped the line. That also made him wonder how much the Borche might move that line over time. No, he didn't like it at all but the advantage he held onto was knowing that they thought they had the upper hand. They were arrogant to a fault and that pride may work in favour of the remnant group of Andromedans, if he played it right.

Following the negotiations with the League of Governors, he, Maneva and Yeovale were given a tour of the city. He was impressed with how they lived. It was simple yet elegant. They wanted for nothing on Terrania. Garon explained that everything was recycled, all their waste including their dead. They didn't bury their people when they died, they composted them. In their minds it was as natural as the cycle of life. What came from the ground went back to the ground. It felt somewhat disturbing to Karlou, and he wondered if it had a long-term impact on their value of life. How could an individual be born, grow up in a nurturing environment, be loved and then die and be discarded? It didn't seem normal but that's how it was done.

All the planet's food and household waste was also recycled. Each family had plots of land for growing food to supplement the large-scale farming complexes that existed outside each city. These people were essentially vegetarian. No animal products were consumed at all, not even milk. They had developed alternatives a long time ago and believed that food from plant life was not only sustainable but much more forgiving on their bodies. Being from a meat-eating race, that might prove a hardship for many of the Andromedans, but Garon suggested it would be a simple adjustment and would just take time. Given the rations they had been eating in recent mons, anything would be an improvement he thought.

He inspected their power grid and was very impressed. Technologically the Terranians were every bit as capable as the Andromedans, to a point anyway but their power systems were exceptional. They used every means to create power, none of which involved polluting the atmosphere with emissions. They had perfected generators that converted oceans waves, river flows and their own star's solar energy into a flawless and consistent power system. All their transport systems were electric too, from their long-haul high speed gravrail systems right down to individual cars although there were very few of the latter. The way the communities were structured, long distance travel was not a necessity for most of the people. The Terranians had adapted to individual community clusters. Karlou wondered how that lack of connection kept everyone on the same path. That question was answered when he visited a school. The education process was intriguing. They didn't just learn mathematics and language; they were classed in the how their society became what it was and how it had to be maintained. At higher levels of education people were tested for their respective level of skill and ultimately chosen for roles that best fulfilled the needs of the community. It appeared that the desires and wants of the individual were very much inferior to the collective needs of the community and everyone was focused on the good of the people and the planet. If there were individuals who simply couldn't meet the necessary criteria to value add to society through disabilities, they were cared for. The Terranian people had overcome all the issues that challenged them, something the Andromedans had barely dinted in their pursuit of peace and prosperity. One thing that Karlou saw more evidence of was the gap between the roles of the males and females, with women being more subservient in every respect. He was concerned by how that might translate to his people should they ultimately settle here.

As Karlou had witnessed from space, the communities ringed the warmest and most fertile parts of the planet, the tropical and sub-tropical zones. All else was left to nature. Animals and plant life were left alone to be what they were meant to be. Hunting was illegal and conservation was key. Karlou asked Garon about the problems of over population and other natural disasters. They were real issues yes, but they were also natural and, where possible, were left to sort themselves out. The only time the people intervened was at times of threat, such as fire or flood. The planet boasted a highly skilled emergency services league which was always prepared to go into action at times of need. That was rare because the planet was in balance but from time to time a major forest fire would threaten a community and it was only then that it was extinguished. Again, Karlou was astonished by their methodology. The Terranians had developed fire suppression systems that were nontoxic and didn't threaten animal or plant life in any way.

But the most impressive thing they were shown, which particularly interested Maneva, was their medical achievement. They had clearly spent many thousands of solar rotations pouring resources into medicine. It had reached a point where the Terranians were disease free and if some new illness arose, which was rare, they could quickly overcome it because they could focus all their resources on one thing. They had overcome everything from cancer, something the Andromedans were aware of, right through to influenza, again an affliction all too common in the Universe it seemed. How they had achieved this wasn't clearly explained but it didn't matter. Karlou was impressed and felt confident that the medical prowess of the Terranians would also be of great aid to the Andromedans. Finding this world was indeed a great piece of good fortune. It was a pity that no one else from their race would ever reap the benefits. One thing did puzzle Karlou, however. When Maneva pressed Garon for answers on the longevity of the Terranian people he didn't put a number on it. He only suggested they were long lived but in comparison to the Andromedan people it was hard to discern who lived longer. Perhaps it wasn't something they felt comfortable talking about. What consequence might it have in any case? Given the near identical anthropological makeup of both races, he was convinced that they could live amongst the Terranians in peace and harmony. Who knows, they may even be able to breed with these people.

Another weird factor noted by Maneva particularly was the sameness of the people. They were all the one race. It appeared that no variation in the people existed anywhere on the planet. The Andromedans had clearly defined races and multiple skin colourings which had developed on their original planet and persisted even after they migrated throughout their system and beyond. Even now, there were white, black, red, brown and yellow skinned people but not on Terrania. When pressed on the anomaly Garon simply said that while they too had coloured people in their distant past, the changes had occurred because of their occupation of the tropical regions of the planet over an extensive period. Their tanned skin was natural. Maneva later suggested to Karlou that recessive genes would have to create throwbacks of different skin colour and other peculiarities of the planets past environs, but she witnessed nothing of the kind. It was very odd but, without a documented history of the planet, who was to know for sure that it wasn't simply a result of a speedy evolution. Nature was tricky that way.

The only other troubling sidenote was the Terranians lack of faith. He didn't understand why they had discarded religion. It was not part of their lives in any way. There were no places of worship. Garon explained that there used to be many religions on Terrania, but they were as much responsible for war and death as anything else, so it was discarded, but why not have one religion like they had one language and one currency? He didn't get it but then why should he? The Andromedans had hundreds of religions, and they bickered and fought endlessly about their respective deities without proving any such beings existed. Blind faith? Perhaps. Maybe the Terranians had that right too.

Reflecting on the tour Karlou thought, *yes, this will do nicely*. No need to take the planet by force which was a relief. They had found their place and they had been welcomed, mostly. He felt good about that.

Karlou went over the possibilities in his head when his communicator buzzed, "Admiral, our transport is here."

"On my way Number 1."

The Borche shuttle was a significant vehicle compared to that of the Andromedans. It had to be to cater for the bulk of each Borche individual. Given the lesser technology the Titania carried, compared to the Borche battle cruiser, the shuttle had to dock with an air lock. The Admiral, Yeovale, Maneva and a detachment of marines traversed the corridor as the Borche seal opened and they were invited inside. They immediately felt the heat from within through their suits. A Borche male simply indicated where they should be seated without a word before the seal closed behind them. They strapped themselves into the oversized seating and the shuttle slid off. The Andromedans made certain they took their own provisions. There was no telling what kind of fare would be on offer during the journey and they were going to be away from Titania for several dars according to Galek.

In a matter of micras they were on board the Quaal and being transported into the depths of the ship, firstly to meet with Galek, "Greeting Karlou. I trust you are well?"

"Yes Galek. I am eager to meet with your clan Lords."

"Excellent. We will be underway shortly. I will have orderlies show you to your quarters. We have sealed off a small section in the ship so that you can relax and not be interrupted. It has been sanitised so you need not fear contracting any illness from us as far as I'm aware and the temperature has been lowered to your standards I hope you will find it comfortable."

"I appreciate that and I'm sure they will be more than adequate Galek."

"Very good. Perhaps when you are settled in, we can meet and talk?" suggested Galek which caught Karlou off guard somewhat.

"Um, yes of course. I would be privileged to do so."

"Very good. Is there anything you need in the meantime?"

"No Galek, we have brought our own provisions. To be honest we don't know what you eat or whether it would be suitable for us, so we thought it best to cater for ourselves. No disrespect."

"Completely understandable. I agree, you may find our diet a little difficult to digest," and Galek appeared to smile although his jaws were certainly quite inflexible, so it looked more like a sneer.

Karlou smiled in return, "Very well. I will see you soon."

"Indeed, I will send for you in approximately one centon. Um, that would be a cycle in your time I would suggest?"

Again, Karlou was surprised, how could he have known the Andromedan time system? No matter, it wasn't a secret in any case, "One cycle. See you then."

With that, orderlies transported the Andromedans to an accommodation section of the ship. There was no shortage of inquisitive eyes upon them as they wound their way through the corridors and tunnels of the battle cruiser. After a relatively short journey they were shown their quarters. As promised, they had the entire section to themselves. They had assumed that everything they did would be under scrutiny, so they kept their talk to incidental topics. Karlou knew it might be suspicious if they didn't discuss the meeting with the clan so they openly talked about their excitement to meet the clan Lords and how good it would be to disarm and find peace at last. Things they hoped would give the Borche no reason to consider them any kind of threat. The accommodation was very basic, and everything was too large, however the extra-large bedding was certainly very inviting compared to their tiny bunks on Titania. Other amenities would require some getting used to such as the squat toilets. Their suits enabled them avoid ablutions for the short term but for this trip, they would need to partake in the use of their host's amenities, which were not designed for the Andromedan anatomy, but they would make do.

Karlou decided on a bolder course of conversation with Maneva, "I must say, I didn't expect to be received in such a positive way. I was anticipating something much more akin to prison transport."

Maneva understood what he was trying to do after he gave her a wink and she followed his lead, "As a military man Karlou, that doesn't surprise me. You assume the worst all the time; do you not?"

"I do but that's because I have spent most of my life fighting against our own kind and then the Borche. It's a natural state of mind for people like me."

"I know," Maneva changed tack, "What do you think will happen when you meet the clan?"

"What will happen? I don't know for sure but I'm hoping I can convince them to agree to the deal we've just made with the Terranian Governors. I would rather that, otherwise we're going to be sent to a place that they will determine, which doesn't entice me."

"Why not?"

Karlou looked at her intensively, "Because when we scanned this region looking for somewhere to escape, we found only one likely planet, Terrania, which means if they're going to recommend something else, it isn't close and may be much less satisfactory. Terrania has everything we need, it's so close in nature to our home world it isn't funny. We couldn't have been luckier. No, Terrania is for us. It must be."

"Perhaps you need to put a bit of faith in the Borche."

"After what happened to our homes and families? That's a lot of faith indeed," the Admiral considered his next remark but then decided to throw caution to the wind, "I'm just not convinced that these Borche can be any different to those we escaped."

"Just like we are all the same perhaps?" suggested Maneva.

"What do you mean?"

"Back home, on our planet and throughout our systems, the diversity of the people was significant, from radical to benign, varying opinions, beliefs that were opposites. Why can't it be the same for the Borche?"

Karlou paused, "You make an interesting point but those are traits of our people. How do we know it will be the same for the Borche?"

"We don't but it might be the case. They said as much."

"Yes, but they may have been saying what they thought we wanted to hear. It could be a total ruse. I will need something more substantial than that."

The Admiral was walking the edge of a cliff with his attitude, but he hoped the Borche, if they were listening, were getting his message. Trust had to be earned.

Maneva thought he might have crossed the line and decided to give him a little reminder of his new role, "Well Karlou, you have thousands of souls to consider, and you are not at war anymore. Remember that!"

Karlou smiled, "The voice of reason as always Maneva. I will do my best, you know I will."

"I do. You're one of the good ones. I'm glad it is you and no-one else in this situation. I very much doubt we would be alive now had any of the other fleet admirals been here."

He smiled again but didn't say anything. Talk soon turned back to Terrania and what it had to offer with its vast areas of land and pristine oceans and forests. The possibilities were exciting. Just one more hurdle to jump, a big one.

Soon after, the Admiral was again received by Galek, this time to talk. Both kept their guards nearby, "Tell me about your people Karlou, where are you from?"

Karlou realised this was an opportune time to hint at his trump card, "Our system is many parsecs from here. We had to make multiple jumps to reach Terrania from the Galaxy of Andromeda, although I suppose the name of it means nothing to you. I suspect you have your own names for the various star systems."

"Indeed, we do but we have substantial star charts, created over thousands of generations of study and travel," Galek explained.

"I see, then perhaps I can point it out. It's not like I'm betraying my people now that the Borche have infiltrated the region and taken possession." The Admiral didn't mind giving Galek a small jibe.

A holographic image appeared in the centre of what was a huge room that looked like a cross between a theatre and a mess hall. The image was spherical and contained endless arrays of star systems and galaxies, "This is the Universe as we know it. We update it with every new discover," Galek pointed and a small red dot appeared within the image, "We are there! Does that help you?"

"This is very impressive Galek. I can see that this would have taken millions of cycles to compile. It's amazing," Karlou studied the holographic images.

"You can walk though it if you wish, it is visible as much from the inside," advised Galek.

"Really?" Karlou stepped into the sphere and was astonished by the view. It was like he had become a God overlooking his creation. He was seeing the Universe from a giant's perspective. He walked to the red dot and looked around, "Can it be magnified?"

"Of course."

"Can you home in on this area," and Karlou indicated a star field that seemed only a short distance from Terrania but was essentially a giant leap in real terms, several in fact. The image stretched out like a balloon blowing up, "Stop! There, that's Andromeda."

Galek leaned forward to observe, "I must say Admiral, you and your people impress me with your achievement and your bravery. Getting here over that kind of space must have been incredibly risky. I'm surprised you made it given your level of technology."

"To be honest Galek, not all of us did make it. We lost a great many of our people on the last jump. I fear they are marooned or gone forever."

"Maybe, maybe not."

Karlou looked at Galek and couldn't screen his own astonishment, "What do you mean?"

"I assume you have the coordinates of that final jump, yes?"

Karlou nodded.

"Well, let's see if we have colonies in the sector who may be able to find your people, or some of them."

"You can do that?"

"Normally yes, but I'm not familiar with that region, it falls outside my dominion, but one of the clan Lords may well be able to assist. I shall ask."

Karlou didn't miss the use of the word dominion but shook it off, he was abuzz with possibilities but then he realised there was no point getting any hopes up. In real terms any such rescue might take eons and that was as good as doing nothing, "Even so Galek, you know what kind of time any such journey might take. It's a very unlikely prospect; perhaps impossible."

"True. We have advanced travel capability but you on the other hand have perfected a jump system that we are yet to crack. If you were prepared to share that with us, we may well be able to create a drive that will enable such a rescue."

Karlou's trump card was already on the table face up it seemed, all the better, "You want our jump drive technology." It wasn't a question.

"Of course."

Karlou again decided not to be diplomatic, "And that's why we are still alive."

Galek didn't answer immediately and looked at Karlou who judged his expression to be one of resignation, but who could tell, "You have been up front with me and so I will do you the same honour, yes, that is why you were allowed to live. Destroying Titania would have destroyed the technology too. We knew you had something special when we found you. A ship such as yours, it did not come here under traditional flight technology, that was easy to determine, so yes, we want your jump drive."

Karlou was fighting his natural urge to lash out, "I see. And how am I supposed to react to that? Knowing that we were to be killed except for a piece of hardware."

"I understand your frustration, but you should perhaps look at the opportunity that has presented itself, you are alive and you have something to negotiate with. I would suggest that you have the advantage."

"You could have just raided our ship and taken it."

"Would you have allowed that?"

Karlou smiled, "Probably not."

"Then you will understand that we, despite your misgivings, are not without mercy."

"But only if there's something in it for you, correct?"

"I believe I confessed that very point. I am not sorry for it. We want what you have, and you want something we can give you. That, to my way of thinking, is a good place to start a negotiation."

Karlou tweaked his chin and pondered for a while, "How can we trust you? Our experience with your kind and now a confession that we were only saved because we had something you desire; they are not grounds for good relations."

"But they are. Think of the two issues separately. Would the Borche you encountered on your World have paused, even if they knew of your technology?" he didn't give Karlou a chance to answer, "I think not. Despite your misgivings, we did. Yes, I admit we would have destroyed you without hesitation had we not detected your drive system, but it saved you and it proved we are not a relentless juggernaut of destruction. You must concede that."

"I understand that, but you expect anyone who is not Borche to bow down to you, disarm and be meek. You possess the systems you inhabit to the detriment of all other species. That isn't something that sits well with me," Karlou said.

"You are wrong. Ask the Terranians. They didn't even know we existed until you came along. We have never interfered with them. Yes, we have watched them, for a very long time. If they posed a threat, that would be different, but they have shown no such tendency since we arrived in the system. Their planet isn't to our liking, so they are of no interest unless they become a threat. That's how it has always been with us."

"So, your existence is based on maintaining superiority in the face of any threat. Peaceful planets are left alone?"

"Yes,"

"And how many peaceful peoples have you encountered?"

Galek appeared to frown, "Very few. Most civilisations are hostile. Thankfully most in this sector are not at all advanced so, we simply watch them, but we have had to eradicate certain threats."

"And if the planet suits you, you will take it to expand your dominion; if it is a threat, you will destroy it?"

"Yes, that is our nature."

"I see, so where does that leave us. We would be considered a threat no doubt and so, should be eradicated based on what you have said."

"Also true, but you have come from afar. You have no home here. These are unique circumstances. There is room for an understanding between us I believe."

"An understanding that involves placing us somewhere that suits you, having us disarm and I would venture to say, give up all our technology?" Karlou asked.

"Mostly yes. Disarm, certainly but some tech would be allowed. Look again at Terrania, a highly advanced race with nothing that threatens us. They have, it appears, created a perfect harmony between themselves and their planet. Some might learn from their ways."

"On that we can agree. So, Terrania, is that on the table for us?"

Galek again frowned, "That remains to be seen, but if you allow me, I can make a case."

"For a price," Karlou added.

Galek simply replied by giving him a sneery smile again.

Chapter 11 – The Deal

For the next several dars the Quaal travelled at twice light speed headed for the second planet of this solar system. The Terranians occupied the third. Both were rocky planets, but they were nothing alike. It surprised Karlou that the Terranians were totally unaware of the Borche presence given their vicinity to Terrania but then, why would they have ever considered the neighbouring planet to be occupied.

The Andromedans kept to themselves, except for the occasional meetings between the Admiral and Galek. Small talk proved difficult as it was clear that the two peoples had little in common. Karlou endeavoured to learn as much as he could about the Borche but had to be careful not to overreach and reveal that he was looking for any new weakness to exploit if necessary. The Andromedan marines carried gelvaps, loaded with lethal fungi spores but were ordered not to deploy them without a direct order from the Admiral. Being totally organic it was thought they would be undetectable unless the Borche tested directly for pathogens. Even so, the fungi were shielded by gel casings so no emissions would be possible and therefore unlikely to be detected by whatever means the Borche employed. That was the hope anyway. Besides, if asked they could simply suggest they were a form of preserved food. Eating one would have no ill effect on any of the Andromedan personnel.

Given the possibility that the Borche may indeed be able to perfect the Titania's jump technology and search for the missing Andromedan armada, an act of aggression now would be ill advised, but the Admiral hadn't yet discarded the idea of an eradication attack when he met with the clan. It would all depend on the results of the 'negotiation.'

As the Quaal approached the Borche home world, Admiral Karlou Vardourn looked upon their planet with trepidation. It was a yellow globe, very cloudy similar in size to Terrania but from what Galek said, most of their water was in the atmosphere. It didn't rain much at all and there were few running rivers, stream or lakes and oceans to speak of. The air was hot and constantly humid thanks to the nearby medium sized yellow star. It made sense that these creatures needed to develop a thick hide to protect themselves from radiation and keep in whatever moisture their bodies required.

The Quaal docked with an orbiting space station, one of several in geostationary orbit. Not only were these staging areas for transport, but they also created a massive defensive grid around, what the Broche called Sennas Beta. This wasn't the original home world of the Borche, Galek said they had been moving through the Universe for so long, few knew of the location of their place of creation, so this world stood as a major catalyst for the Borche here. The Admiral could not help but feel he was being handed a perfect opportunity for payback but brushed off the thought...for the time being.

The Andromedan contingent wasn't given much time to take in the enormity of the space station. After the Quaal docked, they were rushed through to a shuttle bay and loaded straight onto a smaller craft, not unlike the one they had recovered from Terrania. On board was Galek and his immediate entourage. The shuttle dropped through the cloudy upper atmosphere of Sennas Beta and broke through the clouds into open air in just a few millies. When Karlou and the others looked though the portholes they were agog. The light of the yellow star filtered through the atmosphere easily and created a fluorescent hue across the day side of the planet. It was like looking down upon a huge terrarium.

Maneva was starting to understand the elaborate ability of the Borche brain, particularly their eyesight variations. She imagined that the night side would always be semi light given the proximity of star and the way the clouds created the translucent glow. They were clearly adaptable to most environments and despite this not being their original world, it was one they found quite comfortable.

As the shuttle closed in on the surface the occupants could make out a city and lines of what could have been traffic moving in and out, almost a spider web of infrastructure. Another thing that was becoming obvious was the intensity of the heat on this planet, Karlou wondered how long they could manage under its effect before exhaustions laid them low. Galek also became aware of the issue, "Worry not Karlou, we will adjust the air temperature indoors to accommodate you. We can tolerate the cool more than you can tolerate the heat."

"I would venture to say that your definition of cool would still be stifling to us Galek."

"That is probably true," Galek answered.

"So, you have been through this process many times?" Karlou asked.

"That would be a fair appraisal."

Karlou nodded and swept his eyes back towards the planet. The shuttle was very low now and being steered towards a cluster of taller buildings at the centre of the city, "Where are we Galek?"

"This is our capital, Sennas. There are around ten million residents here."

"Ten million?!"

"Give or take," Galek sneered his smile at Karlou.

The Andromedans were clearly taken aback by the revelation, so many Borche.

The shuttle homed in on what was clearly a landing area, and it was obvious now that the city boasted significant air and ground traffic. The variety of craft was astonishing, the Borche going about their daily business no doubt. The way they conducted themselves was indeed 'normal' in terms of how the Andromedans and the Terranians lived. It caught everyone by surprise.

Galek saw Karlou's astonishment, "Not what you were expecting Karlou?"

"I must confess it is not. I hope you won't be offended, but I expected your lifestyle to be more, basic."

Galek chuffed, which was a Borche form of laughter, "We are highly advanced and long ago discarded our natural tendencies and instincts. We have taken full advantage of technology to build an environment for our people. This planet is a testament to that. Our forefathers terraformed it into an environment that would be perfect for our kind. When we found it, it was a very hostile place, much hotter than it is now and completely encased in noxious cloud. It took many lifetimes to create a habitable world, but as you can see, we have done just that."

"Ah," Maneva cooed out loud, "that explains everything. It looked too perfect to be an accidental discover. Your abilities are impressive Galek."

"Thank you doctor. We couldn't do much about the gravity, we are used to much greater forces, but we have adjusted quite well."

The shuttle touched down beside a waiting ground transport. When Karlou and his group stepped off the shuttle craft they immediately felt the intensity of the environment. This planet was stiflingly hot and humid. Galek took a very deep breath and exhaled, "Aaaaaggggghhhhhh, so good to breath the air of home once more. Much better than the concocted atmosphere on the Quaal."

Karlou was glad he was able to breath his own cool air supply, built into his suit. The prospect of filling his lungs with boiling Borche air was not at all appealing. He imagined he would cough up his innards or drown, so thick was the air with moisture. The delegation was ushered onto the ground transport before any of the nearby locals could take a good look at them. Karlou wondered if that was intentional.

They sped off, Karlou all too aware that they were totally at the mercy of their sworn enemy. For all he knew the Titania was now a floating hulk in space, but he was starting to wonder if these Borche were indeed different. They certainly seemed more civilised and as he took in the scenes of their streets, dwellings and businesses he came to feel more comfortable. The swamp things he imagined these beings to be was a complete misnomer. They had societies and commerce, just like the Andromedans and Terranians. They just wanted to live. The only difference was that they vanquished any perceived threat, which Karlou had issue with, but he was in no position to bargain. For now, he had one objective, to get the Clan Lords to agree that he and his people, possibly the last of his race, be allowed to settle on Terrania.

The transport arrived at a gigantically tall building which Galek said was the regional centre of governance for the Clans. Each Clan Lord oversaw a sector of the entire system. Neighbouring sectors had similar management structures and so on. It seemed that the process was ongoing too, given his experience with what he now believed to be a rogue element of Borche who vanquished his people and their home world and other planets, then again maybe that was just how they dealt with a threat. Clearly if a newly discovered planet suited their kind, they took it. Terrania wasn't a world they were keen on. It had too much liquid water and was cold, except for the tropical regions where the people lived. That suited

Karlou just fine and the Terranians agreed there was room for them, so his argument was sound.

On exiting the transport shuttle, they walked a short distance to an elevator. Very few Borche were in the vicinity except for two that appeared to be gardeners or janitors. They looked upon Karlou's group with much interest until Galek caught them and they quickly got back to work. There was a significant hierarchy here too it seemed. No doubt they would start some gossip amongst the Borche about these strange new beings, or perhaps not. The Borche mindset was completely different, and they didn't seem to care about battle casualties, so why care about a handful of strangers in town.

The elevator, like that on the Quaal was extremely fast and they were lifted in no time to a floor at the very heights of the facility. When the door opened, they stepped into an amphitheatre and were surrounded by over fifty Borche clan leaders who sat in a semi-circle along a vast bench positioned high enough to exert superiority over whomever might be facing them. Behind the Clan Lords were thousands more Borche, witnesses or interested spectators Karlou did not know but his heart skipped a beat at the sight and he immediately felt quite uncomfortable. Galek led the Andromedan group to some oversized seating and Karlou and Maneva sat down. The chair legs had been shortened to accommodate the Andromendan's shorter stature, which was a relief. How silly it might have been to sit with their legs dangling in this air. Galek looked to Karlou, gave him a short nod, then climbed a staircase and worked his way along the line of Clan Lords taking the one vacant seat available. Karlou's marines took station at the rear of the staging area and surprisingly were still in possession of their weapons. Karlou thought the Borche overly confident, but then how much damage could a few marines do, given that at least one hundred Borche guardians stood close by in full battle dress.

Galek began the proceedings, "Members of this assembly of Clan Lords, as the clan leader of the Sennas Faction, I present to you Admiral Karlou Vardourn and Doctor Maneva Gantu of the ISS Titania representing the Andromedan people. They have ventured here to escape tyranny at the hands of what I perceive to be a rogue element of Borche, unknown to us. They seek asylum and I call upon the Admiral to address the Clan Lords with his opening remarks."

Karlou and Maneva were somewhat confused and realised they would have to learn as they went. Galek had not briefed them as to the procedures that would be followed which may have been an oversight or a tactical decision. Either way it was too late now, "Greetings and thank you for giving us this audience. We are the remnants of a people who, while not being perfect, were living our lives on many planets within our star systems when we suffered an unprovoked attacked by the Borche who came with overwhelming numbers and unwavering aggression. We had no opportunity to seek amnesty nor was any quarter offered. It became clear quickly that we were to become slaves or be annihilated. Our only recourse was to escape. Thus I was given charge of a fleet and using an unproven jump technology we made our way to this system, which was one of several that were identified as potentially habitable," Karlou paused but no interruption was forthcoming so he continued, "We were unaware of the existence of any intelligent life here and hoped to find a virgin planet upon which to settle our people. Sadly, due to some catastrophic malfunction most of our fleet and our people have been lost. Ours was the only ship that made it to Terrania. I have met with the Terranian League of Governors and negotiated terms to take up residence on their planet, with your blessing of course. We are similar peoples and the planet suits our kind in many ways. It is a good fit for us," Karlou scanned the row of clan leaders to try and read their reaction but it was impossible and he decided to lay it all on the table in one complete statement, "As I have told the Terranian League, I am willing to forgo arms to live in peace on Terrania. I understand that you perceive Terrania as no threat to the Borche and, I hope that will continue should you see fit to meet our terms. All we desire is peace and a future for our people. We are not at all interested in hostility now or in the future. I yield to your will," Karlou was not keen on his last remark, but Maneva felt it was necessary to win Borche support.

A clan leader quickly spoke up, "Salas, of the Gemin clan, this entire episode could easily be resolved with your eradication could it not? Why allow you to reside here given your technical capability. I am concerned that you are indeed a threat."

"With respect, our technical abilities are not a threat, in fact they are potentially beneficial. We have a jump technology that you desire, correct? I am willing to negotiate that."

"We could just take it," suggested another Lord.

"No, you couldn't. My people have been ordered to destroy the drive should any attempt be made to take it from us by force."

"If that be so, then you demonstrate the exact concern I raised,' suggested Salas, "You are a threat."

Karlou needed to think fast and overcome this line of concern, "We were invited here to negotiate a resettlement for my people. As a part of that I am offering you our jump drive technology. I'm making no threats here, but I do not accept that my comments are antagonistic. The drive is our only bargaining chip. Surely you can understand that. My one and only desire is settlement for my people," Karlou cast a suspicious eye towards Galek knowing the drive technology was his idea.

Galek picked up on Karlou's frustration, "Perhaps my Lords, we should accept the Admiral's gesture. This drive technology is something the Borche must have and, despite the limited science the Andromendan's possess, they have achieved something we have not and are willing to hand it over for a place to live and to lay down their arms in the process. This by my estimation deems them no threat."

"But what of the future, asked another Lord, "What is to stop them taking up arms in the future?"

Karlou jumped on the remark, "There are no guarantees in the generations ahead, but I can give you my assurance that, should my people be allowed to settle on Terrania, then we will abide by their will and therefore pose no threat to you. This agreement is already in place pending your confirmation."

The translators were suddenly muted and the Borche delegates clearly articulated thoughts amongst one another. Karlou could not discern what they were saying but it was obvious that a debate was raging. He felt frustrated but he'd made his point, forcefully. He didn't know if that was the right way to do it, but it was too late now. He looked to Maneva who smiled, "What do you think?" he asked.

"I don't know. What else could you say. We were at a disadvantage from the moment we walked in, you had no time to prepare or think. It wasn't fair."

"Perhaps not, but it's their way and we have to go with whatever opportunity or lack of that is offered."

The translators crackled back to life, "We reservedly accept your offer of the drive, disarmament and your resettlement but we are concerned that you will be a negative influence on the Terranian people. How will you guarantee that will not be the case?" asked Galek on behalf of his fellow Lords.

"I believe my presence here is evidence of that. Having been at war with your kind, the most difficult thing to do is appear before you like this and ask for your help. Try to imagine, that should you be in my position? If I am willing to submit to your will and to meet the conditions set by the Terranian people," he said while internally hating every word of it.

"Sadly, we are not convinced. You have already demonstrated your willingness to kill when you eliminated a scientific contingent who were innocent victims of your wrath. What say you to that?"

"We did that, yes, we killed your people, but we were unaware of your existence here at that time and were of the belief that we had been pursued and under threat. It was an act of self-defence to my mind. Our experience with the Borche to that point involved unwavering assault. We feared that had we not killed them; we would have been killed immediately. It was that simple. I can tell you now that we no longer feel that way. I, we, can see that you are different. You could have wiped us out without hesitation when you found the Titania, but you chose to negotiate. I respect that and I hope you respect what our position was under the circumstances," explained Karlou.

"You make a good point I suppose," said one of the delegates, "The loss of our people is regrettable but it would appear your only experience of our kind forced you to act in apparent self-defence," the delegate scanned his colleagues, "I have no issue with the Admiral's actions in that regard."

Again, the translators were muted and the Lords set about discussing their thoughts. This time their debate appeared much less animated which Karlou read as a positive sign. The translators reconnected again in a few millies, "Your honest and forthright approach is refreshing," said Galek, "We agree to your terms. In exchange for your jump technology and full disarmament, you are free to settle your people in the Sennas region. Is that agreeable to you Admiral?"

"Does that include living on Terrania?"

"It does."

"Then we have a deal, Galek. Please accept my gratitude and the thanks of my people."

"Then it is decided. This matter is closed," announced Galek.

With that the translators clicked off, and the delegates began to move off. Galek returned to the stage and approached Karlou, "As I suggested, it was merely a formality. You have achieved something great for your people Karlou."

"I hope you are right Galek, but I am also grateful. Thank you for backing me."

"What are friends for?"

"Indeed," replied Karlou but he had to hold back a doubtful gulp.

Back on the Quall, Karlou sat quietly on his large bunk pondering the events of the day when Maneva walked in. She immediately noticed that he wasn't happy, "Karlou, what's wrong?"

"Don't you think that was too easy? That whole thing was farcical, wasn't it?"

"What do you mean? They agreed to all our terms. This was a win."

"It looks that way, but something doesn't sit right. Is there something we missed? Something we overlooked?" he asked.

"Like what? We have been given the right to live out our lives on a wonderful, peaceful, prosperous planet. We have a future. I can't think of anything better, can you? Stop being an Admiral for a moment and just accept that you gave our people a fresh start," Maneva suggested, her blue eyes catching his with a smile.

"You're right. It's only natural that I'm looking for the trap. It's a military reflex. I am no diplomat."

"Oh, I think you are every bit a diplomat Karlou. Don't sell yourself short. No-one else in the fleet could have achieved what you have today."

"That's nice of you to say," Karlou said with a slight blush.

"So now we ready our people?" Maneva asked.

"Yes. There will be much to arrange. We will have to go through a rigorous quarantine process and the Terranians have offered to screen us for any pathogens that may be a threat. They have long ago managed to rid their planet of all known disease and should be able to do the same for us, so we are indeed stepping into a perfect future it would seem. You may be able to play a part in that as a doctor."

"It's exciting isn't it Karlou; to have a place without war or hatred."

"Yes, it is."

She kissed him on the forehead and then turned and closed the door before reclining on the bunk. She didn't need to explain, and he didn't need to be asked twice.

Chapter 12 – The Transition

Back on the ISS Titania, Admiral Vardourn addressed the crew to explain the most recent developments, "Having met with the Borche Clan Lords I am pleased to announce we have reached an agreement." There were cheers from all parts of the ship, "I know this must come as a surprise given our experience with this race, but it would appear, back home, we were attacked by a rogue element of the Borche and the Borche of this region are slightly less aggressive. That said, had we not developed jump drive technology, I would not be here to tell you any of that. Their approach to life is to extinguish any threat or potential threat without hesitation, so in that regard we should consider ourselves lucky I suppose," The Admiral cleared his throat, "So given our position, our desire to find a new home, our inability to put up a fight that we couldn't win and having a new home at the ready, I have agreed to hand over the jump drive to the Borche and they have in turn agreed to allow us to find haven on Terrania. Both the Borche Clan Lords and Terranian Governors have made it a condition that we must disarm for this agreement to stand." The response to disarmament met with a more subdued approval, "There is much we will have to give up but I believe the gains will outweigh the negatives. These people, the Terranians, live a harmonious life within their environment, have no weapons and are like minded. We must respect their ways and conform. That will include significant dietary changes for some of you. Meat eaters might find that a challenge, but the promise of a disease-free future and a potentially longer life is, I think, worth the price. I'm sure you will ultimately agree," Cheering again from the passageways, "There will be a quarantine process to follow, inoculations and ultimately a repatriation and resettlement process. Short term pain for long term gain. I wish you all God speed. Thank you."

With that the First Officer, Yeovale Darnuth responded, "Three cheers for the Admiral, Hoo-rah, hoo-rah, hoo-rah!"

The Admiral turned to his First Officer, "Yeovale, prepare teams to deal with all the preparations we need to make. Any equipment we can salvage that falls within the agreements should be taken to the planet. I will meet with the League of Governors to discuss our transition."

"Very good sir."

"Jettison anything, we don't need, no point giving the Borche everything. Without Titania, our interceptors will have to go, and our shuttles will become redundant, but they will be good enough to move everyone to the planet's surface. Most everything we can't use should be discarded."

"Sir, yes sir!"

The Admiral then spied the young cadet who had advised him when the Titania ran into trouble during their final jump. She was looking at him intently, "What's your name cadet? I never did ask?"

"Miran Gase sir."

"Miran, you're aware of the agreement we have made with the Borche?"

"Yes sir, you offered them the jump drive in exchange for free passage and guaranteed safety. Despite any misgiving you may have it was a wise decision if I may say so sir."

"Why do you say that?"

"Well sir, I believe the drive will be useless to them in the short term and probably in the long term. It was rudimentary at best and, as we discovered, very unpredictable and volatile. They would be best advised not to go down that path technologically."

"So, you don't believe they will gain anything from the drive?"

"No, they won't sir, especially if we don't include the neutron detonators."

He looked at her in surprise, "I was worried about those too, they are planet killers."

"Do they have to get them sir? The agreement was for the drive only, correct?"

"Yes Miran, that's all we discussed, the drive itself. I never really explained how it worked. They were too intent on getting it, so I didn't have to sell them a pitch. I suppose they were arrogant enough to think they would figure it out themselves."

"In which case all you should deliver is the drive. I would advise discarding the detonators so that they can never fall into the hands of the Borche or anyone else for that matter."

"What of our missing people and ships, discarding the detonators nullifies any hope of them being saved."

Miran gave the Admiral a look that he read as grief, "Sir, we were never going to be able to save them, and neither will the Borche. If they said they could they've sold you false hope, it's just us sir."

The Admiral looked down, pinched his chin and then nodded, "You may be right Miran. Thank you."

"I am right sir and if I may say so, the Borche may not be happy to discover that we've sold them a dud."

Karlou nodded his understanding then looked to his First Officer again, "One more thing Yeovale."

"Sir?"

Karlou took Yeovale aside so that no-one else could hear and spoke to him for only a few millies before Yeovale nodded and started organising the crew for their move to Terrania.

Karlou then contacted the League and gave them the news of the new deal with the Borche and planned to meet with the Governors to discuss settlement plans.

He hastily shuttled down to Terrania and was escorted to see the Governors who were all waiting eagerly, "It is good to see you again Admiral," said Garon, "We are most pleased with the outcome of your meeting with the Borche, please tell us about your deal with them."

Karlou explained the events on the Borche planet, the location of which came as quite a shock to the Governors, "Yes, their world is the next one closer to your star, the second planet, a very hot world indeed. You should be thankful that they find Terrania not to their liking."

"Indeed," said Garon who looked a little nervous, "So the deal is set?"

"Yes, that is the case. The Borche get what they want, we get what we desire, and you get about ten thousand new people to house," Karlou smiled, feeling slightly embarrassed.

"That will not be a problem Karlou. We have already begun preparations. We have set up a quarantine station where our doctors can do a thorough examination of every one of your people. Then will follow inoculations, to protect you from whatever pathogens that may be of risk to you here, if any," Garon explained, "Once the quarantine process is concluded, you and your people will no longer require your suits. The whole affair shouldn't take too long," Then Garon added, "Oh and if you don't object, we insist that the screening include weapons detection. I hope that won't be a problem?"

"Not a problem at all Garon. We are happy to discard everything as agreed," Garon looked particularly pleased, then Karlou said, "We cannot wait to taste fresh food after such a long time on processed rations and reclaimed water," everyone smiled, then Karlou asked, "What of our roles here? Do you have any thoughts in that regard?"

"Well, we have discussed it and, as I understand things, you all have high levels of expertise in many fields, medicine, engineering and so on, these will be of great value. Your military expertise may well be of value too, to train our police for example. We rarely see what you would call conflict but one thing we cannot predict is natural disaster, so your military may well be perfect candidates to occupy those roles, does that sound appealing?" Garon asked.

"Indeed, it does," Karlou paused, "What of my role? How do you see me fitting into the mix?

"That was our first decision and if you are willing, we would offer you a position on the League of Governors as your people's representative. It seems only right. What say you?"

Karlou couldn't hide his astonishment, "You're serious?"

"We are. You are the leader and you are a man who is admired and respected by his people. It was not a difficult decision on our part. I, we, hope you will accept the role."

"I would be honoured but is an appointment proper given your democratic approach?" Karlou wondered.

"Under the circumstances, it is fitting. In time your role will be open to the same electoral processes as ours. In the short term though, given the exceptional circumstances, we feel your appointment is the right way to go."

"Thank you. I will discuss it with my officers and crew. They need to be aware before I can formerly accept."

"We understand. On the matter of housing, we have already begun construction of a series of dwellings here in Genoa. You will all live as a single community at first. Over time your people may decide to venture out and find their own way. This, we feel, will be something that will happen naturally. We do not wish to impose barriers or limitations on any of you. You will be citizens of Terrania and thus have all the rights of the people," Garon said, then added, "But your adherence to our laws is paramount. We must preserve peace and balance, so you must disarm. That said. Many of your personal effects and technology will be welcome here I'm sure, but it will all need to be vetted."

"I understand. My people know that this will be an unusual change to their lifestyles but they're all very excited by the prospect of a peaceful existence, finally rid of conflict."

"Our only concern is that you have all been brought up with an adversarial mindset. Conflict is natural to you. That is something we managed to rid ourselves of a very long time ago. It has taken generations for us to develop and reach a lifestyle consensus; how we should live and maintain peace for ourselves and for the planet. We are concerned that this will be difficult for you and the other Andromedans. What is your feeling on this?"

The other Governors remained quite silent. Clearly Garon had been made the designated negotiator for the transition.

"It is true that our people have known war for much of their lives, but we don't exist for conflict. It's not a conscious choice or a preferred option at all. Yes, we fought between ourselves then fought the Borche. I do think though, that there will be little to antagonise our people as their lives will be full and they will want for nothing, which in our past has been part of the problem, the imbalance of resources and so on," Karlou tried to make the issue sound like a small problem but deep down he really didn't know how some might cope, "Even so I promise you that I will do my very best to keep everyone happy."

"Good, that is all we can ask. In the early stages I would like to offer your people some educational opportunities, to learn about our planet, our lifestyles, our balanced approach to living as a part of the planet and some of the dos and don'ts if you will. I suppose you might call it, um…"

"Orientation?" suggested the Admiral.

"Precisely. We would also like to offer everyone a global tour so they can see what our community is like across the wider region. Would that be of interest?"

"Most definitely. I don't know what to say," Karlou added, "You are being most gracious. We could not have hoped to find such a place to call home. We are humbled by your generosity and acceptance of our kind."

"It is indeed our pleasure Karlou," Garon replied," However there is one thing that we would like to investigate?"

"What is it?" Karlou asked, his curiosity tweaked.

"There is an uncanny similarity between our peoples, I'm sure you'll agree," Karlou nodded, "We are very keen to do some tests to see exactly how similar our people and yours are. It may even be possible for us to cross breed. This could be quite an astonishing discovery don't you think?"

"To be honest Garon, it never crossed my mind. It's an interesting notion indeed. I think though, such a decision needs to be discussed with my medical personnel, if that meets with your approval."

"Of course," Garon answered casually, "You are free people of Terrania now, this is not a demand nor a requirement. It was simply an idea."

"Very good. Thank you."

The meeting continued for some time with discussions covering a myriad of subjects and issues from language, education, food and water to clothing and a few touchy subjects like religion. The Terranians had rejected religion generations back, given its historical significance in many of their global conflicts. The Andromedans however, had true believers in their ranks. How would such a situation be managed? In the end it was decided that religion, having not essentially been banned on Terrania, could be practiced in private by individual personnel but under no circumstances could they recruit disciples or spread their beliefs. While some of them might find that to be counter to their beliefs, the decision was not negotiable. Karlou wondered how such a directive could be policed given the passive lifestyle approach of the Terranians. Time would tell.

Over the next several dars Admiral Karlou Vardourn overwatched the process of stripping down the ISS Titania of all their essentials and transporting them to the planet. The ship was stripped down as much as necessary, leaving little for the Borche to salvage given the deal was for the jump drive only. At the same time, non-essential personnel were transferred to the quarantine station on Terrania and tested for pathogens and inoculated against any potential risks on the planet itself. The Andromedan with the honour of being the first to venture onto the planet's surface without the need of an environment suit was Cadet Miram Gase. Not surprisingly she had volunteered. The Admiral thought her the perfect candidate to test the conditions. On his next visit to the surface, the Admiral met with her to see how she felt, "I'm fine admiral. The air is so pure, at first, I felt dizzy. The oxygen saturation here is a little more significant than we're used to, so it took some time to adjust but our bodies should cope well. It might take a few cycles for our people to adjust but it is a very comfortable environment."

"That's good news. Have you tried any of the local food or water yet?"

"No sir, I'm sticking with our rations for now," Miram explained.

"Well, I see no reason why you shouldn't test the water, so to speak," which brought a smile to Miram's face.

"I will do so at the first opportunity sir."

"Very good, let me know how it goes."

"Yes sir."

Karlou then met up with doctor. Maneva Gantu to check on the transition. She had been stationed in the quarantine unit to assist, "It's going well Karlou. Most of our people are in excellent physical condition and are adjusting quickly. The process should be swift I think."

"What of the injured from the Gravitational wave?"

"They are being cared for and should all fully recover. The medical abilities of the Terranians are beyond anything I could have imagined."

"So, no issues at all?"

"Well, a few, but the Terranian doctors are incredibly capable and have dealt with everything we've come across so far like it was nothing at all."

"Really? Such as?"

"Well, the chief cook was diagnosed with Glioblastoma, a cancer of the brain."

"Oh, my word, what's the prognosis?" asked Karlou, clearly shocked.

"Back home his chances would have been next to nil, but here, he is cured. They have cancer and everything else beaten. They have no illness or disease, and it appears that our physiology is compatible with theirs, so their treatment works for us as well as it does for them."

"That is incredible news Maneva," Karlou said, clearly astonished, but then he looked down and rubbed his chin.

"What is it Karlou, I know that look?"

"The Terranians asked me if we might be interested in a compatibility test, um…" He paused again and Maneva smiled.

"You mean sexual compatibility?"

"Yes! That's what they want to know, but I wasn't sure how to answer. I mean, I can't see the harm, but I didn't want to commit without discussing it with you first," Karlou explained."

"Wise as always Karlou but I don't see any threat in looking at the possibilities and I don't see why we cannot breed with the Terranians. I've had the opportunity to talk at length with some of their doctors and we are essentially the same physically. There are some differences which are simply environmental of course."

"Such as?" Karlou asked.

"Well, we are bigger on average and we have different shades of skin pigment, but these are natural variations. Hair, eyes, those things all vary but they are superficial really."

Karlou pondered once again, "Doesn't that strike you as odd, that we are so much alike in so many ways. I would have thought it impossible to find a near identical species totally separated from our own evolutionary processes?"

"Well not impossible, clearly, but the odds would have to be astronomically against it and yet, here we are," said Maneva.

"How do you explain it?"

"I cannot, except to say that the seeds of life here were probably nearly identical to what happened on our original home world billions of years ago...or..." she now pondered.

"What?"

"The theologians were right," Maneva suggested which raised Karlou's eyebrows, his forehead crumpling into a series of parallel lines,

"Oh, wouldn't that be a coup? That God made us and did it here as well."

"Indeed, and there will be those who will think that is exactly the case," Maneva suggested.

"And who could blame them?"

She looked at Karlou and smiled, "They must have nearly died when they saw you only had four fingers. I can only imagine their first reaction. They must have thought you some weird beast under your suit."

"I did feel a slight recoil when I shook hands for the first time."

"Did you explain it to them?"

"They didn't ask, so no."

"I thought you would have jumped at the chance to tell a few wars wound stories and how you lost your thumb," and Maneva laughed.

"Well maybe it'll come up one day and they can share the joke."

"Needless to say, their doctors are fully aware that we have five fingers on each hand, just like them."

"Indeed," answered Karlou.

Over time, more Andromedans made the transition and settled into their new lodgings and a new life. The speed at which housing was made available was astonishing and the homes were spacious and comfortable compared to the cabins of a war vessel, even one as large as the Titania. For the time being they used their own rations, not only for the sake of extra safety but because it had a shelf life and it seemed pointless to waste good food, bland as it was.

One of the final tasks was to dispose of the jump drive's neutron detonators. They were disarmed, disassembled, the various parts ejected into space in a multitude of directions so they could never be found or recombined. The Borche who were stationed nearby didn't intervene or question their actions. Karlou thought the precaution mute but didn't say anything. He had good reason to allow it. When the Titania was completely stripped and all the equipment transferred to the planet, the skeleton crew, mainly officers, signalled the Borche who hastily arrived to take possession.

Galek came aboard with his entourage of Borche guardians and technical personnel who would take and steer the once grand Titania to the Borche planet where they would not doubt learn as much as they could about, not only about the jump drive but the Andromedans themselves.

"I trust the transfer of your people has gone well Karlou," asked Galek.

"Yes Galek, it has been flawless, and we are excited about our future. Thank you again for your support and trust."

"It will be beneficial to us all, I'm sure."

After an awkward pause the Admiral cleared his throat, "After following through on the agreement, I present to you the ISS Titania, jump drive intact. It is yours to do with as you see fit. She had been a grand vessel and we will miss her. I relinquish all rights and possessions in the name of the Supreme Armada of Andromeda as is my right and in front of these witnesses. She is yours from this moment," the Admiral stated.

"Thank you, Admiral," Galek thought it best to use a formal title under the circumstances, "We take possession of your vessel with gratitude."

"Very well. I don't suppose you require any form of inspection or orientation?"

"That won't be necessary Karlou. Our people are already very much aware of your ship's capabilities and technologies. We will have no trouble at all,'" Galek noted with pride.

Karlou gulped wondering if they were aware of the neutron detonators, but it was too late now, "Very good. In that case we will take our leave. There is but one shuttle on board which we will use to take to the surface and, as agreed, it will be dismantled and destroyed. We will no longer have the capacity to leave the planet, nor wage war."

Galek simply bowed in acknowledgement and Karlou replied with a traditional Andromedan salute; nothing more needed to be said. Karlou and his officers went to the flight deck, boarded the shuttle and launched. As the craft sped away, Karlou took a long last look at the ISS Titania and shed a tear. It was a combination of sadness and satisfaction. He was saying goodbye to a friend but leaving behind a violent past.

Yeovale Darnuth, the First Officer noticed the Admiral's expression, "She served us well Karlou and will do so one more time."

"The Gelvaps are placed?" Karlou asked very quietly so that none of the other officers could hear.

"Yes sir, throughout the ship's ventilation systems."

"And by the time they realise there's a problem, the spores will have been spread far enough to wipe out their entire planet?" Karlou asked.

"That would be the case, yes sir, and ultimately beyond as they travel throughout their systems. Over time it should reach most of their peoples I imagine. It is virulent and fast acting and should achieve one-hundred percent mortality. They simply won't have time to develop a cure," explained Yeovale.

"That's better than they deserve. If I could have used the neutron detonators on their space stations, that would have suited me better, but it would also have been suicide. My only regret is that the Borche who attacked our home world's may avoid the outbreak."

"I wouldn't go that far sir. I don't believe the Borche here to be unaware of the supposed rogues we encountered. It was a convenient denial I think sir."

Karlou nodded, "I tend to agree. Treachery runs deep with the Borche. I wish I could see their faces when they realise what has befallen them."

"Chances are they will never figure out it was intentional, the Gelvaps are well hidden and will ultimately dissolve, leaving no trace. They may just think it an exposure to something we carried naturally. Even if they vent the ship and disinfect it, the Gelvaps will remain in place for a time before breaking down and releasing the fatal dose. Best of all, the vents are too small to crawl through for the Borche, so the odds are highly against any detection at all, visually or otherwise."

"Very good. You have done well Yeovale. If it works, we will have eradicated one of the greatest threats to peace in the Universe."

"It will work sir," Yeovale added with a burst of pride.

"Yeovale my friend, we must never reveal this to anyone. This is between the two of us. This knowledge must die with us, understand?" Karlou whispered.

"Rest assured sir."

Karlou sat quietly for the rest of the trip to the planet's surface, a wry smile on his face. He never trusted the Borche and never believed they would stick to their deal. Any excuse would have seen them turn on the Andromedans and the Terranians for that matter. He had convinced himself that he had no option.

Now he would enjoy peace and prosperity knowing that he had achieved one last great victory.

Chapter 13 – Oversight

Admiral Karlou Vardourn was the last of the Andromedans to complete the transition and take a breath of fresh, open air for the first time in many lunar cycles. He found the air of Terrania to his liking. Like many others, he felt a little lightheaded at first, but his body soon adjusted to the conditions. Balance was a small issue for a while due to the variation in gravity, but it wasn't significant and was easily overcome in a very short time although some made the transition without any ill effects, particularly the younger crew members.

Karlou oversaw the destruction of the Andromedan weapons and the shuttle and interceptor fleets, as was the agreement with the Terranians, and the Borche for that matter. He would have loved to have kept something, but he dared not risk it in case the Borche somehow survived the spore attack. He didn't want them using anything as an excuse to decimate Terrania. So, everything that could be construed as a weapon or transport device was destroyed. In the end Karlou felt deeply satisfied. He may well have duped the Borche, but he had no such issue with the Terranians and wanted to meet with their every wish to guarantee the future of his people.

Their community in the city of Genova was welcomed by the local people, and they intermingled without any hint of animosity or suspicion. The Andromedans, for all intents and purposes, were treated with respect and in turn learned to let their guard down and to accept the local hospitality. As most of them were military personnel, it wasn't an easy task to turn off their alert instincts, but it would get easier in time.

As the Andromedan rations ultimately started to run low, people began to try the local fare. Most agreed the food was very good, simple in most respects but much more appealing than the military gruel they had been eating for so long.

Karlou attended his first assembly as a Governor of his people, an appointment that his entire crew endorsed. He took his place at the table alongside Garon, with whom he had struck up a friendship.

Percius of Eropa opened the dialogue, "Welcome to you all. It is a significant moment in our history as we formerly welcome a new Governor to our ranks, the representative of Andromeda, Karlou Vardourn," and he gestured towards Karlou with a slight bow in recognition of his standing. All the governors clenched fists and hammered the table in a gesture of acceptance and congratulations.

Percius continued, "We hope your time here is rewarding and well spent. You have much to do for your people as they settle into life here. It is indeed an exciting time." He looked around the table to all those seated, "As is our custom, I now call on the newest Governor to address the League formally for the first time."

Fists again pounded the table and voices echoed their support, "Oh yay!"

Karlou stood and acknowledged the Governors as the echoes of support died out, "Thank you, I am humbled by your acceptance of me and of my people. I do very much hope we can repay your generosity in time to come."

"Oh yay!"

"I know there has been much discussion and negotiation about our arrival and subsequent settlement on Terrania. It goes well so far, and our people are beginning to settle into their new lives. It will, of course, take time to adjust to so many changes, the air, the gravity, the language and so on. Thank goodness for translation technology," the Governors laughed, "but in time I hope we can all learn your language so that we may feel more a part of this society."

The governors all listened intently as the electronic scribe kept an official record of proceedings, "I suppose the time has come to tell you of our journey in more detail. You are aware of the reasons, the attack on our many planets by the Borche in the Andromeda Galaxy. We lived on seven different worlds, all consumed by the Borche. Our only option was to flee. We did so with little time, sending seven fleets to seven different worlds that were identified as 'liveable', including Terrania," Karlou looked around but no-one interrupted; they were mesmerized by his words, "We had to use experimental jump drive technology to make the journey and were almost here when catastrophe struck, spreading and perhaps destroying a significant part of our fleet, the final jump failed. It seems that there is no chance we will ever see them again. Somehow though, we found ourselves on your doorstep by a stroke of good fortune it seems."

He cleared his throat and then continued, "By way of understanding us I should talk about our people before we became explorers of the Universe. Our species originated on one small world, not unlike this one, a blue planet with vast oceans and continents, a beautiful world I am told, a planet our ancestors called Earth in the Milky Way galaxy. Our people, over many thousands of what were called years, venture all over the galaxy and occupied a multitude of worlds, then spread beyond that galaxy to Andromeda. The people of our original world may still exist, and we could have tried to find them as a part of our escape from the Borche, but it was thought that they would have already succumbed to the Borche, being so close to Andromeda, or in travelling there we may have exposed them to the threat. It seemed prudent to avoid such a risk and put as much space between us and the Borche as possible. As you now know, the Borche exist in greater numbers than anyone could have imagined."

Once again Karlou looked upon the Governors who hadn't wavered in their interest, "We are known as Homo sapiens, descended from the great apes of the planet Earth but we are generally referred to as humans. Our evolution has been very much akin to yours, so much so that, according to my medical personnel, the only differences between us and the people of this planet are purely environmental. We are essentially the same," he paused and took a deep breath, "You may wonder how this is so, and I cannot answer except to say that the recipe that caused life to explode on Earth originally must have been of the same broth that brought forth life here.

Perhaps, not long after the big bang, our worlds mixed at some level and there followed a series of events that spawned our independent, yet near identical evolutions. Clearly this will be the subject of much speculation and study going forward."

Karlou decided not to include the religious theories that had been raised within discussions amongst the Andromedans given the Terranian feeling on the subject, "I will conclude by saying that we feel very fortunate to have found you and even more fortunate to have been accepted into your society as equals. I will work hard to ensure that we are cohesive, productive and peaceful members of this world forever more, thank you."

The governors all stood and hammered their fists into their palms in appreciation.

Galek responded on behalf of the governors when they resumed their seats, "Karlou of Andromeda, your words have fascinated and intrigued us and yes, there is so much we can learn from one another. Our people once ventured to the stars as well, but we never settled beyond this planet. Why, I do not know but perhaps in time we will understand that too. We congratulate you and your people on their resilience and bravery under extreme duress. You are here because you showed the kind of resolve needed to overcome adversity. This is something we greatly respect and are proud to have as part of our cultural future. I look forward to many, um, years of cooperation and learning between our peoples."

"Oh yay," came the cries of support from the Governors.

Galek continued, "You are most welcome to investigate our history. Our archives will reveal that our history is much like yours, even down to our distant ancestry. We too evolved from a form of primate, so it is believed."

"That's fascinating. I would very much like to investigate that. Thank you," answered Karlou.

Galek smile and nodded approvingly as Percius took the floor, "So, to the business of the day…."

One thing Karlou wondered about was the lack of female representation. Perhaps it was a coincidence and for now it wasn't his greatest concern, but he made a mental note. The meeting then worked through a strict agenda, much of it surrounding the transition of the Andromedans into Terranian society but also dealing with issues from around the globe. The planet and its people, despite peace and prosperity, still had to deal with once force that couldn't be controlled, nature. Issues of drought, flood, fire and pestilence were all on the agenda but the way the Terranians dealt with it was extraordinary. The fallout was dealt with through a widespread support network, a fully integrated cooperative approach to sustaining life and balance on a planet wide scale. If drought affected one area, it was left to nature while another zone covered the shortages and supported the effected people until the environment cycled back to normal again. The approach was a perfect synergy between the people and the environment. Everything was recycled; nothing was wasted. Even the people, when they died, were returned to the environment to benefit the living through a composting system. The Terranians didn't see any problem with this, it was their way of completing the cycle of life. Being without religion, it had no impact.

In restoring balance to the world in generations past, most problems were short lived and when intervention was necessary, it was expedient and designed to have little impact. Fire was indeed the major concern while floods were mostly mitigated in the population areas. Famine and disease simply didn't exist. Economically the approach was simple, one currency and one economy. There was no greed, no hostile multinational system of ownership or profit, it simply wasn't in the mindset of the people. They all lived and worked for each other. That, Karlou though, might be the most difficult thing for his people to get used to. Humans had always operated on an adversarial level economically. Personal wealth was the goal of every human being. On Terrania, that simply didn't exist. Here a cleaner was valued as highly as a governor, no-one looked down on anyone.

Karlou listened intently and answered questions occasionally but didn't engage in the local issues. He didn't yet feel qualified to do so but hoped to eventually be as much a part of the conversation as everyone else sitting around the table. He gleaned that all were very astute, but it was becoming apparent that the vast majority of Terranians highly evolved intellectually. As he sat, he glanced at a glass of water which had been left for him, as was the case for everyone else. He picked up the glass an examined it closely; the contents were clear, and cool to the touch, as you would expect. He hadn't yet consumed anything outside their own rations but realised that, at this moment, he had no reason to avoid it any longer. Without thinking about why, he sniffed the water, odourless as it should be, he then took the glass to his lips and took a sip. He immediately coughed, not because it was bad but because it was sweet, sweeter than anything he'd ever tasted before. It was unusual but not in a negative way. It was water, pure and clean.

After the meeting, Karlou spent some time chatting with the other Governors, getting to know them and partaking in some of the planets many delights. He found the food to be delicious and most enjoyable. He was surprised to learn that it was all wholesome and nutritious, even down to the little cakes and chocolates. Nothing was processed; all food was plant based and naturally sweetened to a limited degree. Food was designed to be good for the body but also to be enjoyed. The Terranians again had demonstrated their prowess by creating a perfect balance between the body and diet. Karlou had already noted that obesity was not a problem here, all Terranians were fit and healthy.

After the meeting and subsequent post meeting supper, he bid his fellow governors farewell and took the electric light transporter back to the Andromedan section of Genova. He was impressed with the simplicity and speed of the system. Walking was highly encouraged so most people found a short walk after their commute to be enjoyable. Karlou struggled somewhat, having been locked up on a spaceship for so long but he knew he would overcome that in time and regain a high degree of fitness.

Even so he enjoyed the stroll, the sunshine was warm, a bit on the humid side but he only perspired slightly. He took a deep breath and tasted the air. It was pure and he smiled.

On arrival at the Andromedan housing complex he went to the lounge to meet with Maneva and get an update on the transition, "How goes it?"

"Quite well, nothing to report. Everyone feels good and are settling into their homes. The welcome packs include clothing and money. The Terranians have been most accommodating and some of the personnel have already found jobs."

"Really? Firefighting would be my guess?"

"Yes, and some in the departments that look after natural resources. They're all very excited too," Maneva added.

"I'm not surprised. They should do well I think."

"Yes, I think so too," Maneva changed the subject, "Have you tried the food yet Karlou?"

"Yes, just now after the meeting. I cannot describe how wonderful it is. And the water, it has a sweetness to it that I've never noticed in our own water."

"I'm guessing your pallet is simply reacting to the swill we had on the Titania for all that time though," and she laughed out loud.

"I'm, sure you're right. It won't be long before our own rations are depleted so we might as well get used to the local cuisine."

"True, I find the food quite satisfying. No ill effects and easy to digest," Maneva said sounding very much like a doctor rather than a foodie, "Most that have tried it say the same thing. They're not even complaining about the lack of meat."

"Well, that's good news. I thought that might be a difficult change to accept. I imagined that some might go out hunting, but without weapons that might have been a difficult task," added Karlou.

"Does it feel strange not having guns?"

"Yes, I've had one on my hip since I was a cadet. I feel naked without it but I'm glad. To have a future where such things aren't needed will be a relief. I think we all feel like that."

"Good."

Karlou look at Maneva, "Tell me, have you found out anything about the Terranian lifespan? I realise we are going to benefit from their science and can expect to live longer lives, but how long do they live on average? Do you know?"

"Oh, that's the exciting part, without disease and the sophistication of their emergency medicine, the people live to a ripe old age."

He gave her a half smile, "You're taking to a politician now you know, that wasn't an answer, give me a number."

Maneva laughed, "You a politician, who'd have thought? Ok, considering that they have a totally different system of time I'll have to convert, um, ok, so I figure...."

"Stop playing games, you already know the answer," Karlou declared.

Maneva laughed again. She'd tried to toy with him, but he saw straight through it, "Ok, no more games. Their lifespan is between six or seven hundred solar quarters!" She was now talking in terms of the Terranian time system he noticed.

"What? That's more almost treble our life span!"

"Yes, they are very long lived."

"What does that mean for us?" Karlou asked excitedly.

"Well, we have not had the advantage of being native to this world so we should not expect any such extension to our lives, but I would guess that most can expect to live fifty percent longer, maybe a bit more. Perhaps the younger people will gain a greater benefit."

"That's extraordinary. I would never have thought it possible. As a military man, I always expected to live a short life with a violent demise. This will take some getting used it," Karlou suggested clearly overawed by the prognosis.

Maneva nodded in agreement, "It will be a wait and see situation. We won't really know for a long time, but we can all expect to feel good for most of the rest of our lives, barring injury. There's no cure for misadventure."

"True."

They sat and chatted for a long while, both feeling incredible relief to at last be settling down and starting over. Their personal fondness for one another would no doubt be able to flourish as well.

In the fullness of time, the Andromedans became increasingly accustomed to their new home. Many ventured out, started creating friendships with the locals, visiting business centres, shops, galleries, museums and enjoying the pristine environment. Genova had a large central park and lake system to provide sanctuary for the people. It was well patronised by the Andromedans. Some even took to swimming, something they hadn't been able to do for an incredibly long time.

One thing they all had to get used to was the variation in time. Terrania's day was quite a bit shorter than the home planets. Given that the Andromedans came from seven different worlds in their home system, the variations were no great impost to some who travelled between planets regularly. Others struggled significantly. Many took to calling it space lag, but time would sort itself out. Learning the terminology and local calendar was going to be a necessity as well as the issue of clocks, dates and places. It was a lot to take in but would eventually become natural.

Over the course of the next solar quarter, the Andromedan food supplies were finally exhausted. Several had already dispensed with it and were eating Terranian fare full time. When the Andromedan water supply was gone, they tapped the local system to replenish their needs. Everyone agreed the local water tasted sweet and refreshing.

But soon after, people began to complain that they felt dizzy and soon many Andromedans suffered the same affliction. It prompted Maneva Gantu to bring it to the attention of Karlou, "I can't explain it, people are dizzy. I don't know why."

"Could it be the food?" Karlou suggested.

"I don't think do. There's nothing toxic about it. The plant life here is as palatable as anything back home."

"What about the water or the oxygen saturation?"

"Maybe. There might be an additive in the water that we're net familiar with. It's probably something we'll get used to."

"I'm not concerned," added Karlou, "We always knew there would be some minor problems. It will pass."

"I'm sure you're right."

But it didn't pass. As time went on the number of people complaining about dizziness grew until every Andromedan was afflicted. Karlou held an emergency meeting with the League of Governors, "Our people are suffering some kind of reaction to something on Terrania. We think it might be the water, but we cannot be sure. I would like to ask if there is some additive that we're unaware of? Some kind of chemical perhaps?"

The head of the Water Resources Department, Janeth was present along with several other departmental directors. He answered, "We do not add anything to the water. We prefer to use it in its natural state. It is tested regularly for purity but given that it is drawn from the cleanest aquifers; we haven't had any issues for a very long time."

"Could there be something else?" Karlou asked in desperation then added, "Our doctors have not been able to find anything as yet."

Another director spoke up, he didn't identify himself by name, "Our quality control is of the highest order regarding all consumables. I doubt you will find that the issue relates to the food, the air or the water. I would suggest that perhaps something else has affected your people, perhaps while you were on your ship, something which you have carried with you and is now starting to manifest itself."

Karlou then remembered the Gelvaps and wondered if they might be the problem. If so, it might prove catastrophic. Could they have all been infected? Would it spread to the Terranian population? "Thank you for your candour. I do not mean to make accusations; I am simply trying to get to the bottom of the problem. It is impacting on all our people."

"I am very sorry to hear that Karlou," said Garon who squirmed at the news, "Rest assured we will do everything in our power to assist. May I suggest we gather some of your people and do some tests, with our own physicians?"

"That would be most welcome, thank you. Do you mind if the Andromedan doctors assist? They may well be able to come up with something too."

"Of course. This is something we should all solve together but please don't be alarmed. I'm certain that it is a simple and solvable problem," Garon added giving Karlou a reassuring nod.

"I hope you are right Garon and thank you again."

Several Andromedans were tested by a series of doctors, both Terranian and Andromedan. Blood tests, faecal tests, swabs, skin samples, hair samples and urine were all taken and rigorously tested but after many rotations of testing, nothing obvious came to the fore.

Karlou met secretly with Yeovale Darnuth, his former First Officer to confront his suspicions, "Do you think this could be a result of deploying the Gelvaps Yeovale?"

"I don't know sir. You might be better off asking Maneva but if they work the way I was told, wouldn't I be feeling worse than everyone else? I was the one who placed them and was most exposed. I do not feel any worse than everyone else."

"Perhaps you are of a stronger constitution Yeovale."

"Maybe so, but I do think it's something to ask Maneva."

"Thank you, I will."

Karlou took a short walk to see the doctor and stumbled slightly as a dizzy spell impacted on his ability to balance. He knew immediately that it wasn't an issue with the gravity, he too was afflicted by the mystery ailment, and it was getting worse. He waited a moment until he felt a little better before stepping into Maneva's new office. She noticed him immediately, "Karlou. Oh my, are you alright?"

"I'll be fine. It's just a dizzy spell."

"Sit down and rest," and she ushered him to a lounge, "tell me what's happening."

"No time for that, I need to ask you a serious question."

"What is it?" she wondered.

"The Gelvaps, could they have leaked or released the spores sooner than we thought?"

"Of course not. They were made under strict security and couldn't have been active until deployed. The containment systems are flawless, so no chance of that."

"What if they were released? Could they then create an issue for us?"

She looked at his suspiciously, "What are you saying?"

"Nothing, I'm just trying to find an answer, just like you. Could a gelvap be the problem if it leaked or broke or something?"

"No. They are species specific. Nothing in them can possibly impact on us. They were created to target..." she paused and looked at Karlou again, this time with a hint of horror, "You deployed them, to kill the Borche. They were released?!"

He didn't answer, he simply looked down at the floor and nodded.

"How. I oversaw their destruction myself?"

"You destroyed fakes."

"What?"

"We never returned them after visiting the Borche ship. We replaced them with ration blocks from the galley, just in case we needed them. They looked similar and we didn't think you'd pay much attention."

Maneva cried in anguish, "You know what they will do? It's genocide!" Maneva screamed.

"I know and I don't care. What they did to us was the same thing. They have no right to assert their will on the Universe and dictate how people should or shouldn't live. They need to be wiped out and that's what will happen!"

"Oh my God! I can't believe you did it...and I was a party to it. I gave that to you." Maneva crumpled to the floor, the realisation of her involvement, unwitting as it was, too much to handle.

Karlou wanted to console her, but he was still dizzy and would fall too if he moved, "I'm sorry, but the war never ended with them, and I had a weapon and I decided to use it. Good riddance," he coughed.

She didn't answer. They both sat silently for a long time until Maneva finally stood up, "I'll do some tests to see if the Gelvaps have somehow infected us."

"Thank you," said Karlou.

"How are you feeling?" she asked.

"Much better."

"Good, now leave"

He looked at her face and saw an anger in her features he'd never witnessed. He nodded again, "Ok. Please tell me what you learn," and he stepped into the corridor as the door slammed behind him.

Chapter 14 – The Horrible Truth

Over the next several cycles Terranian doctors reported that all their tests came up negative. There was nothing in the food, water or the atmosphere that could be identified as a cause of the symptoms being experienced by the Andromedans and no such affliction was occurring in the indigenous people. It was unique to the Andromedans.

The results narrowed the likely cause down to only one thing and again suspicion focussed on the Gelvaps. Maneva, still seething from the revelation that the weapon she created had been deployed, tested several personnel including Yeovale Darnuth. If the Gelvaps were the cause, she would find evidence in the human respiratory system. The spores were released as the Gelvaps evaporated and were designed to be inhaled where they set about growing and ultimately killing their host. As they did so they would multiply and be exhaled to infect other victims. In short, a Borche would quickly succumb to respiratory failure via an inability to oxygenate their blood. An early symptom would indeed be dizziness.

She conducted x-rays, stress tests and breathing tests. She took biopsies of lung tissue and ran culture tests on respiratory fluids. It all took time and she was exhausted but after checking and rechecking the results she finally took her report to Karlou. She walked into his office without knocking and found him staring at a computer screen reading some kind of report. He swung around and saw her, a look of doom on his face, "We've suffered our first casualty. The cadet, the first one to complete the transition, she died a little while ago. They'll conduct a postmortem, which may give us something."

He was clearly shaken by the news and Maneva's mood softened a little, "I have the results you've been waiting for."

Karlou snapped out of his sombre state for a moment, his features revealing a ray of hope and expectation, "Well?"

"I can confirm that there is no sign of anything affecting our people that can be connected with the Gelvaps."

"Are you certain? It was our very last theory."

"I am certain. The spores cannot affect us. They never could."

Karlou slumped in his chair, "And the Terranian doctors are no closer to solving this. There is literally nothing wrong with any of their processes that could be a reason for our affliction."

"I know. So, what do we do now?"

"We keep looking. One death is too many. Let's not make it two!"

"Right then," and Maneva turned to leave but then stopped, "You know, we may be looking in the wrong place."

"What do you mean?"

"Well, we're looking for something in the food or in the water. What if it's not a thing within a thing but the thing itself?"

"You sound like you're practising a tongue twister, what do you mean?"

"What if the planet itself is making us sick, the whole planet? What if it's rejecting us like your body rejects a foreign organism?" Maneva suggested.

"Sounds like science fiction. How could a whole planet be rejecting a human being?"

"Just a thought. What else have we got to go on?"

"True," and Karlou pinched his chin in deep thought.

Maneva looked at him and could see he was under a great deal of pressure, they all were but she had to address the issue that was not receding in her mind, "You know, when this is all over, I don't know how I'll ever forgive you for what you did." Karlou looked at her and was about to speak but she gestured for him not to interrupt, "You betrayed my trust and made me a part of something too horrible to contemplate. I'll need time to process it, but I may never get past it. You should be ready for that."

He looked her in the eye and nodded again, "I understand and for what's it's worth, I'm sorry I got you involved. I regret that, but I don't regret killing an enemy. I'll never regret that."

"I know, but it may have cost you something even greater."

"What's that?"

"Me." And with that Maneva left.

As the days went by the symptoms worsened and the death toll rose. It had reached a crisis point. The cause had to be identified quickly so that any hope of a cure could be devised, if it was at all possible. Another disturbing discovery was that there were several pregnant women within the Andromedan population, they all miscarried regardless of term.

While postmortems on the deceased adults proved fruitless, the Terranian doctors were keen to investigate the terminated embryos and infants to see if there might be clues in their cells. This proved more difficult than anyone expected with grieving mothers reluctant to allow their stillborns to be cut up and examined. The human attachment to the dead was demonstrably different to that of the Terranians and something the local doctors had trouble understanding. Maneva Gantu had to work some diplomatic magic to keep the humans calm. She was ultimately able to gain the approval of two of the mothers to give up their children for examination.

The Terranian doctors quickly examined the two foetuses right down to a molecular level and made an extraordinary discovery. Both babies had suffered catastrophic cellular destruction. In short, their bodies were unable to grow because the cell division or mitosis required to enable that process had failed. A further examination of several adult bodies showed signs of a similar affliction, their bodies had systematically failed to repair damaged cells. The deaths were caused by a physical breakdown in the mitotic spindles. In other words, their bodies stopped regenerating new cells.

Maneva discussed the issue with her team and with Karlou, "Now that we know what's happening we can look for the cause. There are so many that are now so weak they cannot get out of bed or eat, it's likely we'll lose many before this is solved."

Karlou looked haggard, no doubt a combination of stress and his own body not functioning as it should, "Can we find any commonality between those that are suffering more?"

"What do you mean?"

"Well, what if the people who are on the verge of death have been more exposed to the source than the rest of us. Can we investigate what they've been doing? Where they've been working. Focus on the worst cases and see if there's any similarity in their actions?"

Maneva pondered momentarily, "It's a good theory. We'll interview as many as we can. All the critical cases are being cared for in the same section of the hospital."

"Good. Let me know what you learn."

"Of course, Karlou," she looked him over and said, "You need to rest, you look terrible."

"I can't rest. This is all because of me. I must see it through."

"A few micras of sleep won't do you any harm."

He nodded but didn't say any more. Maneva left and rushed to the hospital to talk to anyone who was strong enough to convey a lucid thought. Initially she didn't hear anything that seemed remotely connected to the problem. No-one seemed to have anything in common with anyone else. Age didn't seem to be a factor with the young as affected as those nearing middle age. There were no elderly people on Titania, very few in the fleet overall. It was thought the original seven fleets would be more likely to succeed with a younger population. That didn't seem to matter now.

Maneva conducted a dozen interviews and finally happened across a young engineer. She asked him the same question she'd asked everyone else, "Where have you been and what have you been doing?"

He struggled to speak but was able to talk, albeit slowly, "I've been working on the water distribution network. It's not that different from what we had on Titania, just over a city sized network."

"When did you start to notice symptoms?"

"Within a few dars of starting the job."

"What changed, do you know?"

"Aside from where I ate my meals, nothing really," he explained.

"So, you primarily had your meals in our community?"

"Almost exclusively until our rations ran out."

Maneva thought for a moment, "And the symptoms only started after you stopped eating our rations?"

"That's right. I was perfectly fine until then," explained the engineer.

"Hmmm, that doesn't help me. We've all experienced that. Is there anything at all that you've noticed that's different?" Maneva asked feeling desperate.

"What do you mean?"

"I don't know; I'm grasping at straws here. I'm just trying to find the thing we're missing. There's a commonality that might be right in front of us and we just can't see it."

"Well, I don't know about that, I'm just a glorified plumber."

"I know, I'm sorry to put all this on you," Maneva added.

"That's ok, I want to help any way I can."

She was about to move to the next patient but decided to chat a while to lift his spirits if she could, "How do you like your job?"

"I love it. The Terranian people have been so nice. I guess the only thing I struggle with is getting used to their terminology. Even with translators, there are some things that puzzle me."

"Mm? Like what?" she asked without really focussing on the topic.

"Well, the signs, I can't read them, so they have to verbally translate everything, you know, intake valve, valve stopper, things like that."

"I can imagine."

The engineer frowned as he forced out his next sentence, "The weird thing is they keep using the term D2O. I say to them; 'you mean H2O, right?' But they're adamant that it's D2O. It's funny really. The translation for water doesn't work."

Maneva looked at the engineer, eyes wide open now, "Wait a minute, their definition of water is D2O?"

"Yeah, it's weird right?"

Maneva's face drained of colour as the realisation materialised, "Oh my God!" and she sped off before the engineer could ask what all the fuss was about.

She sprinted as best she could to her office, double checked a few things then went directly to Karlou's office where she found him asleep on his office lounge, Karlou!"

He jumped with a start, "Wha…what is it?"

"It's the water!"

"Huh? What?!"

"Wake up Karlou. I know what's wrong, it's the water! The problem is the water," Maneva yelled.

"Karlou shook himself into full consciousness, "We've already tested it, there's nothing in the water, no contaminants."

"It's not something *in* the water it *is* the water. The water is the problem. It's D2O," she blurted.

"What? I thought water was H2O, what's D2O?"

"It's heavy water Karlou, not the water we know."

"You mean radioactive water, like nuclear heavy water?"

"No, it's nothing like that, it's natural, but it's not H2O, it's deuterium!" she explained.

"Wait a minute. I thought water was water, why is it different here?"

"I've checked and looked at some articles in our archives, it's very rare in the Universe. H2O is predominantly the water you'll find almost everywhere. That's what fostered life on all the planets we've inhabited and every other one where water has been found, just not this one."

"Ok, how is it here and nowhere else?" Karlou asked.

"Planetary scientists believe that water was deposited by comets, most carrying H2O, but around 2% of water as we know it contains deuterium, which is harmless at that level BUT many think that there could have been comets that might have deposited D2O in some parts of the Universe and it looks like we've found one. Terrania is a D2O planet," Maneva explained but he noted she didn't appear positive about the revelation.

"So, you're telling me there are two kinds of natural water?"

"Yes!"

"And I'm guessing by your expression that this isn't an easy fix?"

Maneva looked down and shook her head but couldn't say the words that were swirling around in her brain.

"Maneva? What is it?"

"There's nothing we can do to fix this; the D20 will kill us, all of us."

"What?! Why?" Karlou asked with bewilderment.

"Our species, all life as we know it has grown and evolved from H2O, it's the common denominator. Our bodies, our ability to exist and to function are all based on H2O as the fuel of life right down to how our cells grow. D20 won't work for us. It's like putting the wrong fuel in a shuttle. It will cough and splutter for a while but then it will fail. That's what's happening to us."

"But everything looks so normal here. How can it be bad?"

"Because it's not water as we know it. The Terranians and all other life here evolved in this environment. This is normal to them but to us it's poison. As the deuterium replaces the H2O in our bodies we will fail too," said Maneva.

Karlou was speechless. He had no words and just stared at Maneva with a gaping mouth. The silence was palpable until he finally said, "So, there's nothing we can do?"

"Short of finding a permanent H20 source or relocating, no."

The colour, what was left of it, drained from Karlou's face, "How did we miss this?"

"We never considered it. We just assumed it was water. It never crossed our minds, why would it?" answered Maneva, a tear running down her cheek.

"How long have we got?" Karlou asked.

"Hard to say, a dozen cycles, maybe more, maybe less. Not long at all," she revealed.

"And how quickly will those Gelvaps take to kill the Borche?"

Maneva was startled by the question, "Um, hard to say."

"I need a number!"

"Oh, um, it would be quick. They have no defence against it. They would be overwhelmed by it quickly, from infection to death in a few dars. Why?"

"Could you cure it?"

"The fungus? I don't know. Time would be the problem."

He didn't answer to that, but he did ask, "Can you get Yeovale for me?"

"Yes of course," and she went in search of the First Officer.

Karlou was desperate but he knew there was one change left to save his people. A very remote and improbable chance but he had no alternative but to try.

Maneva returned in quick time with Yeovale. Karlou told her to explain what she'd learned, which she did. The shock on his face was evident in the creases across his forehead.

Karlou then said, "We need to contact the Borche."

"What?" asked Yeovale.

"We must contact then now and ask them for help. We need to get off this planet!"

Yeovale quickly realised he was right, "We can use the terrestrial communicator we sent to the League."

"Yes, get it and do it fast," Karlou added.

"Yes sir," Yeovale said as he caught Maneva's eye. She knew what he was thinking. It might be too late regardless. The Borche could well be done for.

The unit was retrieved and set up in the Andromedan compound. Technicians connected it to a large antenna array salvaged from Titania. Karlou recorded a short but succinct message, and it was transmitted as soon at the Borche planet rose above the horizon in the evening sky...

'This is Admiral Karlou Vardourn on behalf of the people of Andromeda on the planet Terrania. We seek an audience with The Borche to discuss a growing problem on this planet. We believe the issue confronting us may be a shared experience and so, we would hope to work together to find a solution. We await your reply. There is little time.'

Karlou lied but he believed that this approach would be the best way of, not only getting their attention, but motivating them to come to Terrania. He would sort out the details later, perhaps. The message was beamed out to Sennas Beta repeatedly in the hope of a response. Personnel listened around the clock for a reply.

"How long do we wait? Asked Yeovale after a frustrating few dars of silence.

"As long as it takes," suggested Karlou, "but I fear that it might be too late and even if they are able. They may have realised we are the cause of their affliction and refuse to help."

"And then?"

"We die Yeovale. It's that simple. This D2O problem isn't something that can be remedied with a pill or an operation. It goes right down to our DNA. We cannot exist in this environment," Karlou explained.

"I know; I have seen what is happening to people. They have gone from dizzy, to losing their babies to literally unravelling cell by cell. Since we announced the D2O problem people have stopped eating and drinking to try and stem the effects but that is counter-productive; they're simply delaying the inevitable."

"What are our losses now?"

"Approaching one hundred Sir and that will accelerate I fear," Yeovale added.

"How's morale?"

"Bad sir."

At that moment a young officer interrupted, "Sir, we have a reply!"

Karlou and Yeovale rushed to the transmitter. Karlou put on a headset and clicked the transmit button, "This is Karlou Vardourn, with whom am I speaking?"

Given the distances involved the message took around 53 millies to reach Sennas Beta and around the same time for them to return a signal. It was a painstaking way to communicate.

"Karlou, this is Galek," he sounded very tired and quite weak, "We are sorry to hear of your plight, but I fear there is little we can do to assist. As you have gleaned, we too have been struck down by a mysterious infection. It ravages our people. We are powerless to combat it for now; our doctors cannot find the source nor can they treat it. Its effects are swift. Are you of the opinion that it is the same affliction you suffer?"

"Hello Galek. I cannot be certain, but it may be so. I am hopeful that we can work together to find a remedy. Unfortunately, we have no way of getting to you. You have our ship and our transports have been destroyed. Even so, they would not have the fuel to reach you in any case. You must come to us."

The messages between the two had to be long winded or the conversation would have been much more cumbersome and frustrating. Long, detailed dialogue one way and the same back again, cramming information into every transmission.

"You were hasty in following the conditions of our deal Karlou, but I admire that you were willing to adhere to the request. I had my doubts. We may be able to put together a skeleton crew on the Quaal and attempt to get to you, but it will be on the condition that you will be assisting us with a cure. Have you learned anything?"

Karlou realised he might get away with a half-truth, but it would in no way be of any assistance to the Borche, "We know what is ailing us here and we believe we have a solution. I would hope that it can assist you too." It was a total fabrication in real terms, but these were desperate times.

Galek responded with a question, "If you know what the problem is, why do you require our assistance? Surely you own doctors and the Terranians can deal with it locally."

Karlou realised he may have gone too far. He'd inadvertently revealed a flaw in his story. The question needed to be answered but he didn't know what to say. Galek was an astute individual and wouldn't be easily blindsided.

Yeovale suggested and Karlou flicked the transmitter again, "We believe that the problem occurred because of the damage to Titania resulting in a pathogen from one of our med labs breaching the ventilation systems. We brought it with us to Terrania and, it would seem, you too have been exposed. My senior doctor, Maneva Gantu is of the opinion that we may be able to test the pathogen and develop a cure if we can get on board Titania and find a sample."

It seemed plausible. He hoped Galek would consider it more than a coincidence that both groups were suffering a mystery affliction at the same time and thus, accept the probability.

Galek responded, "We have been all over your ship and found nothing. What makes you think otherwise?"

"There is no other explanation, Galek. This is the only likely cause and the only course of action for both of our peoples it to allow my doctors access to Titania. We know the ship much better than you and we can get into places your people cannot," Karlou insisted, knowing the last point to be a solid fact.

There was a long delay which could only mean a deep discussion was taking place between the Borche leadership, then, "Very well. We'll spool up the Quall and send for you. We'll signal when we arrive."

Karlou let out a sigh of relief and transmitted his thanks then added, "You're worth your weight in water Galek." He'd said it without thought; it was an old Human saying after all.

It may have been a mistake, or it may have been a calculated response, but Galek's reply set off alarm bells as soon as Karlou heard it, "Not if it's the water, you're drinking Karlou. See you soon."

He dropped the headset and sat stunned for a moment. He thought of the ease with which the Borche had agreed to their settling here, the fact that Borche scientists were on Terrania when they arrived and the statement by Galek that Terrania did not suit their needs. He was led to believe it was too cold, but it wasn't that, it was the water. The Borche knew it! And their insistence that the Andromedans disarm and disable all potential space travel was a convenient way of trapping them here. He'd followed that directive, more the sake of the Terranians than the Borche. Consequently, they had no way of leaving the planet which was exactly what the Borche wanted. Now, with death certain for the Borche and Andromedans, they needed each other. Such irony. Karlou just hoped that the Borche were fit enough to make the journey to Terrania.

Over the next few dars the radio remained silent and the death toll grew. After a few more dars Karlou again attempted to contact Galek but received no reply. In desperation he hailed his own fleet, in the vague hope that someone would hear it but even if they did, how could they get to Terrania in time if at all. He recalled the comments of the young cadet who was adamant that they were all lost and he began to weep.

The doctors, human and Terranian worked feverishly for a remedy, but it was pointless. Terrania was a poison planet and was systematically killing off the new arrivals. As time passed more Andromedans died. Karlou believed that the League of Governors and all the doctors and scientists did everything they could to save his people but, ultimately, there was nothing they could do.

Soon Admiral Karlou Vardourn was too weak to raise his head and as Maneva soothed him with kind words he passed with a long last breath, tears trickling down his temples. Maneva believed his final thoughts were of self-loathing and regret for failing his people, failing his mission and his duty but mostly for failing as a Human being.

Within the next few Terranian rotations the death rate accelerated alarmingly until finally the entire population of the Andromedan people were gone. Help never came, not from the Borche and not from their own fleet. It was likely the Borche suffered a similar fate, wiped out by the Andromedans who were in turned wiped out by something as innocent as water.

The desperate move to escape the Borche and find a new world was, in the end a tragedy, sealed by hatred, revenge and plain bad luck.

The Terranians collected the dead one by one and disposed of them in their tradition way, giving back to their planet. At least the Andromedans would contribute something, albeit as fertiliser.

The League of Governors considered the events of the last several solar quarters and resolved to be more vigilant in future. These events were indeed troubling and unforeseen.

As more time passed the people of Terrania returned to normal life and while none would soon forget the Andromedans, eventually they became a part of history.

Epilogue

As Admiral Karlou Vardourn sat before the Borche Clan Lords on Sennas Beta pleading his case for asylum on the planet Terrania, a contingent of three Borche appeared again before the Terranian League of Governors with an ultimatum.

The Governors had already agreed to offer asylum to the Andromedans but only if the Borche agreed to a deal to hand over the ISS Titania and it's jump drive technology, but for the Borche that wasn't enough.

The Borche representative crackled his remarks through the translation technology and his metallic voice sounded harsh and direct, "We are here to make certain that you follow through on your deal with the Andromedans; that you will ensure they gain asylum here."

Garon of Estonita had somehow become the spokesman for the League in all matters involving the Andromedans and responded, "We have made a deal with the Andromedans as you are aware, but it is dependent on the outcome of the negotiations with your Clan Lords."

"The Andromedans will be granted all they request, that is certain," suggested the Borche representative.

Garon frowned, "Then I don't understand, why do you need to address the issue with us?"

"We need your guarantee that they will be disarmed and that their ships will be destroyed. They must never be allowed to leave this world. Can you make certain of that?" added the Borche male.

"Well, we have already made our position clear and they have agreed. What more can we do?"

"Your people are all too willing to take the word of Admiral Vardourn at face value, but we know these humans better than you do. They are violent and unscrupulous. They will try to hide things from you, weapons, drugs, perhaps even a transporter. This cannot happen," demanded the Borche delegate.

"You sound very certain," Garon said in surprise, "but we haven't seen this characteristic. They seem more than willing to meet our requirements and live by our laws."

Even though no-one could see the Borche faces through their shielding, they were clearly frustrated, "We have had dealings with these humans previously, fought against them on their home worlds and know of their tendencies. You would be best advised to vet them thoroughly during the transition or we will need to take steps for ourselves," the intensity of his voice was unmistakable.

Garon and the Governors all reacted with shock, "What does that mean?"

"We have been watching you for a very long time. You are no threat to us and that is why your planet has been left alone. That and its environment. We could not live here even if we did find it desirable," explained the Borche.

"Because of the climate, it's too cold," Garon suggested.

"That is only a minor issue. Your planet is unique and the only one we know of in the Universe. Because of that, we cannot live here."

Garon's and the governors were confused by the statement, "We don't understand, what do you mean?"

The Borche speaker brushed off the question, "It matters not. The Andromedans think we do not care for our people like they care for their own. On that they are wrong, but we are happy to let them think that is the case. We cannot waste Borche lives assaulting their ship when we can get what we need by agreeing to a deal here."

Garon looked at his fellow Governor, but no one had words for a moment then he said, "Are you asking us to be party to some kind of conspiracy?"

"Yes! They can never know of this meeting. They must disarm and destroy all weapons and transports, and you must oversee it! Your silence on this issue must be guaranteed. No-one outside this room is to be made aware of this meeting. Am I clear?"

"And if we don't agree?" Garon asked glibly.

The Borche speaker held a gaze at Garon for a few secs for effect, "We could simply wipe you out but the Clan Lords feel it would be better at this juncture to suggest that we simply tell the Andromedans of your 'other' policies if you need motivation, the policies you have, we suspect, not shared with Admiral Vardourn and his people. I imagine such a revelation will not sit well with them."

Garon gulped and feigned ignorance, "What policies?"

"Please Garon, I can see through your body heat that you know exactly what I am talking about. The inferior status of your women for one thing but moreover your cleansing policy designed to maintain purity of your race. I wonder how you will deal with the many variations of Andromedan peoples? Their coloured skins, their politics, their religion. It must abhor you deeply," the speaker suggested.

Again, Garon and the Governors were agog, "How did you come to know all this?"

"As I said, we have been watching you, very closely, it matters not how," answered the Borche, "I wonder how you were planning to ultimately deal with the Andromedans after they settled here. We know you don't have the capacity to turn them away and I suspect they would have taken land by force regardless. So how would it feel to have *mixed* generations of Terranians born here? That must be eating you from within, is it not?"

Garon's face went from one of shock to a scowl of contempt; he could no longer conceal the truth. He looked directly at the Borche speaker, "We were prepared to let this generation live out their lives but render them incapable of breeding. We have the medical ability to do it without their knowledge. There will be no future generations!" Then he added, "And, our policies are rendered pre-birth, it is not like we're killing our people in the streets."

"I understand that, but it is of no concern to us how you and your people choose to live," Then the Borche speaker returned to the subject at hand, "I can tell the Clan Lords that you are willing to meet our demands?"

Garon didn't have to look to his fellow governors, he simply nodded, "Yes. We will make certain that the Andromedans can never leave the planet and that their weapons are destroyed. You have our word."

"That's good, we are pleased and remember, we will be watching," said the speaker but before he turned to leave, "One more thing, you will have to continue to act as if you are fully cooperating with them, assisting in every way possible. Make them feel quite at home. Allow your people to welcome them, become friends, give them work. The Andromedans and your own people should not suspect anything. Do you understand?"

"Why is it so imperative that they cannot leave?" Garon asked.

"You will no doubt learn that for yourselves in time, do we have a deal?"

"Yes!"

The meeting ended without another word.

Sanita finished putting the children to bed and walked back into the kitchen where she found Filo, deep in thought, "What is it, Filo?"

"I was just thinking about the Andromedans. They came here looking for a hope and a future and died for it."

"Was there nothing anyone could have done Filo?" Sanita asked.

"No, but it's been a big wake up for the Governors."

"What do you mean?" Sanita asked.

"The Astronomical Society has been given authorisation to increase monitoring for external signals now. We should be able to build bigger antenna systems and listen deeper than ever before."

"That explains all the new equipment upstairs," she said giving him a steely look, "but why would the League need to do that?"

"We now know there are at least two species of alien out there, perhaps more. They are intelligent and dangerous. The Governors believe we need to be aware of any future threats."

"I see, but what could we possibly do if someone or something turns up again. We are incapable of stopping them. That has become clear," Sanita suggested.

"It's true that we have no armed forces, but we have science," Filo said earnestly.

"What are we going to do, throw beakers at them?" Sanita added with a laugh.

Filo didn't take kindly to the jibe, "Of course not. We will learn about them, find out what they want and open our doors peacefully."

"That doesn't sound scientific Filo."

"It's not, the science comes next. We secretly find out what hurts them and we act on that."

"What do you mean?"

Filo was getting frustrated, "I mean that the League of Governors doesn't want to be caught off guard again."

"And how do we achieve that? Yes, it was a surprise indeed to have aliens on our doorstep, but the Andromedans posed no threat, they only wanted to live in peace."

"You are so naive Sanita, it's little wonder that our females don't hold positions beyond the household on Terrania," Sanita didn't react. Then Filo added, "The Andromedans were aggressive and war like. Just coming here wouldn't change that. It took us thousands of generations to get to where we are. The Governors believe it would only have been a matter of time before they threatened our way of life. We couldn't let them breed and grow in numbers; there were simply too many of them to maintain a balance and when their population grew, we would have faced major problems in the rotations ahead. Our numbers are strictly controlled, as you know," Filo explained.

"I am fully aware of how things work here. I'm a little shocked at learning of how the Governors felt about the Andromedans but I understand the reasons. So how did we do it?"

"The solution was built in. They couldn't survive here; our water was not the same as theirs."

"You mean the D20?" Sanita suggested.

"Yes; deuterium, heavy hydrogen. They are a race that evolved from H2O. As soon as they started drinking our water and eating our food, their bodies started to fail. Their own water was replaced by ours and initially it would have seemed ok, but over time they would have noticed dizziness, then their bodies would start to fail as more D2O replaced their own fluids. Once they reached 25%, they were sterile and the pregnant women miscarried. At 50% they died."

"My word, that's incredible, how do you know all this?" Sanita asked more in astonishment than horror.

"Garon told me, he says we were very lucky."

"Why do you say lucky?"

"Because Sanita, this planet is unique. Our water doesn't seem to exist anywhere else in the Universe. That means most extra-terrestrial life was created through H20. Anything that tries to establish itself here will fail. The Borche knew that that's why they didn't want to take our planet. We have an inbuilt immunity," Filo explained with a beaming smile.

"They could have just attacked and left us for dead. That seems to be their way of fixing things from what I have heard."

"And they surely would have, but the Governors did a deal that ensured our safety. We would trap the Andromedans here by making them give up their weapons and transports. The Borche would be rid of a problem and so would we."

"And we can trust the Borche?"

"Of course not, but from what I've been told, that's no longer a problem either," Filo said.

"Really? Why not?"

Filo smiled again, "One of the Andromedan officers told our doctors about a fungus that was left on the ship they gave to the Borche. It was released through the ventilation ducts and from all reports was very effective."

"So, the Borche are dead too?"

"Yes, Jako has been observing, what the Borche call Sennas Beta and reported it inactive. They are most certainly dead."

"My goodness! Two races wiped out. It's so terribly sad."

"We were no supposed to know any of this but with the Borche gone, we can now know the whole truth and moreover live without fear," Filo then said, "The Andromedans dealt with the Borche, and nature did the rest for us."

Sanita was quiet for a moment then looked at Filo and said, "You know, it might just be easier, if there is a next time, to just to tell the aliens that we have deuterium and that might just resolve any future issues. They won't want to live here."

Filo looked at her, bemusement on his face but said nothing while Sanita smiled at him with some level of satisfaction.

They finished cleaning up the kitchen and sat watching their entertainment screen for a while until Sanita got sleepy, "I think I'll go to bed Filo. Will you be coming?"

"Not yet, I'm wide awake. I might go up to do some observing. There's lots to learn out there."

She smiled and gave him a kiss on the cheek, "Don't stay up too late."

"I won't."

"Goodnight Filo," said Sanita as she slipped off to the bedroom.

Filo climbed to his roof observatory and smiled at the sight of his new equipment. His listening and observing gear were ten times better than he'd ever had before and the new quantum computers were exceptionally fast and capable of hundreds of thousands of calculations per sec. He was giddy with excitement at the prospect of making new discoveries.

He fired up the equipment, set the antenna array towards a designated section of space that had been allocated to him and sat back with his headset on and listened to the strange and beautiful radio waves emanating from the Universe. It was a sound he very much enjoyed.

He must have been more tired than he thought because in a few mins he was asleep. Suddenly his slumber was disrupted by an electric crackle, and he jumped with a start as a voice burst from the headphones on the Low F Band,

"This is Cion Zanaeus Captain of the ISS Vittorius, First Andromedan Fleet, we received your message Admiral, please respond."

END

Other publications by Andrew Dunkley are available through most retailers and online distributors in paperback and eBook formats.

All I See Is Mud

5 Irons Don't Float

Parallax

<u>Contact information</u>

You can email Andrew via alliseeismud@gmail.com

www.ingramcontent.com/pod-product-compliance
Lightning Source LLC
Chambersburg PA
CBHW071522110726
47908CB00003B/923